THE BURNING PLAIN

THE BURNING PLAIN

Ruth Janaway

Chivers Press
Bath, England •
Thorndike Press
Waterville, Maine USA

This Large Print edition is published by Chivers Press, England, and by Thorndike Press, USA.

Published in 2003 in the U.K. by arrangement with the author c/o Juliet Burton Literary Agency.

Published in 2003 in the U.S. by arrangement with Ruth Wilson.

U.K. Hardcover ISBN 0–7540–8832–4 (Chivers Large Print)
U.S. Softcover   ISBN 0–7862–4881–5 (Nightingale Series Edition)

The text of this Large Print edition is unabridged.
Other aspects of the book may vary from the original edition.

Set in 16 pt. New Times Roman.

Printed in Great Britain on acid-free paper.

British Library Cataloguing in Publication Data available

Library of Congress Control Number : 2002111647

CHAPTER ONE

Sir George Denton looked at his daughter and said formally, 'James Brunswick has just asked for your hand in marriage, Alexandra. You have not known each other very long, but I understand that you favour his proposal.'

He had been closeted with James for two hours while his daughter sat in nail-biting suspense, straining every nerve for a hint of the conversation in the library—the conversation that would affect the rest of her life. His voice gave no indication as to his decision, but the use of her full name told how seriously he was considering the matter.

Her throat was dry when she answered. 'Yes, Papa, I do! And we've known each other for eight weeks. We met at Edwina's coming-out ball. James has been in constant attendance ever since and a frequent visitor to the house.'

Sir George adopted his favourite stance before the fireplace. His brown eyes fixed intently upon his daughter and she looked fearfully back at him. An ex-military man, he had never hidden his suspicion of 'civils' such as James.

'Well, he seems a fairly decent man,' he admitted finally. 'But his lifestyle is vastly different to yours, Alexa.'

1

'I'm aware of it, Papa, but there's little he hasn't told us of himself.'

'So I've noticed,' Sir George said drily. He gazed down at his wife who sat beside the fire, her golden head bent over the tapestry that was growing steadily beneath her skilful hands. His brow wrinkled in a slight frown. 'James is thirty eight years old—considerably your senior.'

'An age gap is no bar to happiness, Papa,' Alexa cried in swift defence. 'You are older than Mama by fifteen years and there couldn't be a happier couple!'

Lady Emma Denton looked up, smiling ruefully. 'She has us there, George!'

Neither parent mentioned that if Alexa were to marry James Brunswick, she must travel to India with him, the country she had always yearned to re-visit. Nor did they caution her to examine her motives carefully.

What Sir George did say was, 'I suppose the age difference is not necessarily a bad thing. James has an established career, a respected position and financial security. Achievements often sadly lacking in the young jackanapes of today.'

The approval was somewhat grudging but it gave Alexa hope.

'Then we have your blessing, Papa?' she asked.

Sir George lifted his coat tails, the better to enjoy the heat from the fire, and sighed. Lady

Emma looked up again and the two exchanged one of their special glances. When she bent once more over the tapestry frame they were both smiling! It was done! Alexandra Jane Denton was betrothed to James Albert Brunswick, a servant of the East India Company presently stationed at Meerut, in northern India.

Alexa rose and ran to her father, but he caught her shoulders, fending off the embrace, and planted a kiss on her forehead.

She turned to her mother who murmured, 'Congratulations, my dear,' and offered a smooth cheek to be kissed.

'James is waiting in the library!' Sir George said. He consulted his timepiece. 'It's very late—but you may have a few minutes before he leaves.'

Alexa needed no further bidding, but in the library doorway she hesitated, taken with a sudden shyness. This was the first time she had been truly alone with James. Dancing in a crowded ballroom was the nearest they had come to privacy, but it had been enough for them to fall in love, for James to propose and be accepted.

Unaware of her presence, he stood beside the fireplace, tall and straight, one forearm resting casually on the mantel. His light-brown hair shone in the firelight and his austere profile was perfectly etched against the dark panelling. Alexa thought how handsome he

3

was, how distinguished he looked.

James sensed her presence and turned. He seemed as over-awed by the occasion as Alexa herself, and she felt a sharp disappointment that he didn't immediately open his arms to her. But that was silly for there was no reason to suppose that James wouldn't prove a true romantic once they were wed. Under that reserved exterior she sensed a deeper, warmer nature not obvious at casual acquaintance.

Her unchaperoned presence told him what he wanted to know, but he asked anyway. 'Your father has consented? You'll still have me, Alexa?'

She smiled, her dark eyes gleaming in the soft light. 'Yes, and yes, James!'

His eyes brightened and he said softly, 'Then I'm a very happy man for we are now betrothed!'

She went to him then, her slippered feet eager, her taffeta skirts rustling richly in the silence of the room. He reached for her, clasping her shoulders in almost perfect imitation of her papa. He bent his head and his lips were warm upon hers for several seconds before withdrawing. It was, Alexa decided, not very satisfactory for a first-ever kiss, but it would no doubt improve. It would be fun being Mrs James Brunswick and free to practise such things.

James took a small box from his pocket and opened it. A thick, gold band set with rubies, emeralds and diamonds sparkled in the lamplight. 'It's a family heirloom,' he said proudly. 'My dear, late mother wore it and it will make me so happy to see you wear it now!' Taking her left hand, he slid it on to her finger.

Alexa stared at it in dismay. The ring was obviously valuable, but far too large and heavy for her hand. She had dreamed of a diamond solitaire, or perhaps sapphires—something modern—but James was looking so pleased that she felt ungrateful and hadn't the heart to object.

There was a clatter of hooves in the street outside. 'That will be my cab,' James said with a grimace. 'I'm sorry I came so late. I didn't allow sufficient time for Sir George to reminisce on the Punjab and the North West Frontier!'

She laughed gaily. 'You should know that an old soldier can never resist the opportunity to re-fight past campaigns!'

His smile was rueful. 'I'm usually happy to talk with your father, but tonight was an exception.'

With his arm about her slender waist, they walked into the hall. 'I'll come earlier tomorrow,' he promised. 'There'll be much to discuss. My leave is up in four weeks time. Not much time to arrange a wedding—and a double cabin!'

Alexa was glad of the shadows that hid the sudden colour that flooded her cheeks.

Knowing Papa, the whole thing will be managed with military precision,' she said lightly, and for a moment he looked puzzled. Humour, she had found, was not James's strong point.

They stopped under the gas lamp, the yellow flame burnishing Alexa's dark hair. He touched her cheek lightly. 'You're very beautiful, Alexa, and you've made me very happy tonight!' His pale-blue eyes crinkled in a smile, his face suddenly boyish as they lost the years in the shadows.

'Dear James!' she whispered and it seemed that he would kiss her again, but the drawing-room door opened and her parents came into the hall with words of congratulation. James gingerly kissed Lady Emma's cheek then shook Sir George's hand.

Neville appeared from the dark recesses of the servants' stairs with a promptness that told of years of military training. The butler helped James with his cloak and handed him his hat and cane before opening the door.

Alexa hoped that James would kiss her again, for that one kiss in the library was nowhere near enough but, intimidated perhaps by Sir George's domineering personality that seemed to quail even the bravest heart, he didn't. His smile, though, was especially warm as he said good-night and took his leave.

Only then did Alexa feel true elation! She was betrothed to a handsome and attentive man whom she loved as he loved her—and would go at last to India! She wanted to laugh, to cry, to dance with happiness.

'You looked flushed, Alexa,' her mother remarked. 'I think bed is called for. There's been enough excitement for one evening!'

As Alexa kissed her mother good-night, she asked a little anxiously, 'You do like James, don't you, Mama?'

'He seems very pleasant, dear! Most suitable!' Lady Emma squeezed her daughter's hand. 'Now off you go! There'll be much to do tomorrow!'

Alexa rose on tip-toes to kiss her father's cheek, weathered by twenty years of sub-tropical suns. 'You are happy for me, Papa? You do approve of James?'

'I wouldn't consent otherwise. James has his feet firmly upon the promotion ladder. He'll provide you with a good home and a secure future.'

It wasn't quite what Alexa wanted to hear. She felt suddenly deflated. Everything seemed so—ordinary! She had always imagined a vastly different reaction to the news of her engagement. Laughter, celebration—but mostly joy tinged with sadness that they would so soon lose their only child. Such emotions would not have come amiss tonight. But Alexa accepted that this stilted praise was the best she would get . . .

She lay awake a long time, savouring her

happiness, picturing the beautiful dress she would wear at her wedding, selecting bridesmaids, listing guests. The ceremony would take place in the beautiful old church of St Saviour's in Whitmore Square, the reception here at the house. The honeymoon would be spent aboard ship on the long voyage to India.

As Mrs James Brunswick she would return to the country of her birth. Although born in the hill-station of Simla, Alexa had only distant memories of India. The family had returned to England when she was eight, after Sir George had been wounded in a skirmish on the Frontier. During his recuperation, his father, Sir Oswald Denton, had died and as the sole heir, George had left the army to manage the estate.

Alexa never tired of hearing stories of India from her parents and their ex-Army friends, and also from Neville who had been Sir George's batman and had followed him into civilian life. Stories coloured by nostalgia and distance, but Alexa had breathed them in until she was filled with a great desire to return to that vast subcontinent.

How fortunate, she thought, that she had fallen in love with James and he with her. The difference in their ages would not prove a barrier to their happiness. James looked younger than his years, came of good family and was undeniably handsome. And as his wife, she would accompany him to India!

Next morning, Alexa hurried downstairs for she had slept late. Neville was in the hall. 'Good-morning, Miss Alexa. There is a gentleman to see you. He is in the small parlour—'

Alexa didn't wait for more. It could only be James! But so early? Was something wrong? She ran along the hallway to the back of the house, the tap of her feet and the swish of her gown disturbing the early-morning silence.

A man was standing at the window looking out, his broad shoulders blocking the light. Sensing her presence, he turned. He wasn't handsome in the conventional way. The planes of his face looked as if they had been chiselled from wood. It was the face of a pirate, a buccaneer, at home on a heaving deck beneath a jolly roger. An exotic face—devastatingly attractive.

Alexa caught her breath. She didn't know who the visitor was, but it certainly wasn't James!

The man's lips moved in the suggestion of a smile. His eyes, Alexa noticed, were the colour of wood-smoke and they roved her person as though she were a prize about to be captured.

'Miss Alexandra Denton?' His voice was deep and rich as the voice of such a big man should be.

'I am Miss Denton,' she confirmed. 'The butter said you wished to see me.'

'I'm here at the request of Mr James Brunswick. May I introduce myself? Lieutenant Gideon Masters of the 9th Lancers, Queen's Royal Light Dragoons.'

'How do you do,' Alexa said weakly and offered her hand.

He engulfed it in his own and raised it to his lips in an extravagant gesture, and his smoky eyes seemed to laugh at her.

Alexa felt herself blush and snatched away her hand, annoyed with herself as well as with the visitor. 'You are a friend of James's?'

'We met on the ship coming home and we are staying at the same club. He asked me to calf and tell you that he's been unexpectedly summonsed to the East India Company offices and expects to be detained for most of the day.'

A little frown furrowed her brow. 'Did he say what it was about?'

'I'm afraid not! Only that he will call as soon as he's free to do so!'

'I see! Thank you, lieutenant.' She failed to hide her disappointment.

'If there is anything I can do, please ask.' His eyes examined her again. 'To be candid, you're much younger than I expected, Miss Denton!'

Alexa elevated her nose. 'Youth, sir, is not a crime!'

His wide mouth quirked in amusement rather than apology.

'I'm afraid social etiquette isn't my strong point. I've been too long in India. My manners are rusty.'

Belatedly aware that her own manners had been forgotten, Alexa invited him to sit down. 'Have you had breakfast, Lieutenant Masters?'

'An hour since, thank you!'

'Coffee, then?'

'That would be pleasant!' His smile was warm and conspiratorial as though they were already good friends and the formal manners a game they played.

She blushed and hurriedly excused herself and went into the hall where Neville hovered. She ordered refreshment for the visitor, then she followed the appetising aroma of fried bacon to the breakfast room.

Sir George had already left for a shooting party in Essex, and Lady Emma blankly refused to entertain a visitor at so early an hour. 'You'll have to see to him yourself, Alexa. He's here on James's behalf, after all. Make small talk until he goes. With the servants about, it will be quite proper!'

Alexa went back doubtfully to the parlour. She wasn't at all sure that anything connected with Lieutenant Gideon Masters would ever be quite proper. And he was far too—too dangerous for a lone girl to make small talk with.

The visitor had resumed his position at the window. Alexa paused in the doorway studying

11

him. Younger than James and taller, his shoulders broad enough to block the light, he looked as solid and as immovable as an oak. He seemed to fill the little parlour and she felt his attraction like a magnet.

'You have a charming garden. Lots of colour for the time of year. My grandmother would be most interested to know how it's done.' He spoke without turning and she wondered how he had known she was there.

'I'm afraid you must ask the gardener, lieutenant!'

She stayed near the door, politely waiting for him to go, but he seemed oblivious and went back to contemplating the garden.

Finally, tiring of his rudeness, she said, 'Please excuse me, but I must go out soon. I have much to do.'

He turned to face her. 'I'm at your service. Where shall I drive you?'

'Where . . . ? Did James . . . ?' Alexa bit her lip, wondering how to get rid of this persistent visitor. 'You're very kind, but it will be some time before I'm ready,' she said firmly. 'Besides, I'm sure your wife will be missing your company.'

A light danced in his eyes as he smiled down at her. 'The only Mrs Masters I know of is my grandmother and as I've already spent six weeks at her home, I'm sure she'll be pleased to spare me.'

Alexa resisted the temptation to smile back.

Drat the fellow! Why didn't he leave? But, as he was here at James's request, there was little she could do. He seemed a fixture in the little parlour and after a brief hesitation, she surrendered and went up to her room to change.

CHAPTER TWO

The morning was crisp and clear with a hint of frost in the air. Park Lane and Oxford Street were thronged with people making the most of the pale sunshine. The costermongers were out in force and Alexa wrinkled her nose in appreciation at the smell of toasted muffins and roasting chestnuts.

Risking a glance at her companion, she found that he was watching her with a smile of admiration and she looked away quickly.

Leaving the carriage, Gideon Masters accompanied her into the scented interior of a dressmaker's salon where she collected the evening gown previously ordered by her mother, and then into the drapers where she purchased half-a-dozen pairs of kid gloves for her father.

'Where would you like to go now?' Lieutenant Masters asked.

'Hatton Garden, please—if you are sure you have time to drive me. I don't want to keep you from more important things.'

'Miss Denton, I can think of nothing more important than driving out with you. Time and I are yours to command.'

Alexa tossed her head, sure he was teasing her. She dared not look at him for if he was smiling she was afraid she would smile, too, and that would be disastrous. She didn't want to form a rapport with this too-attractive escort.

In Hatton Garden, they entered a jeweller's shop and arranged for Alexa's engagement ring to be made smaller. It was not the design of her choice, but she had decided not to ask for another. Her preference seemed petty when compared to the pleasure it would give James to see her wearing it.

'Will it take long to alter?' she asked the jeweller.

'If you can leave it three days, madam. It is a delicate job, for the settings must not be disturbed when the gold is removed.'

'That will be quite all right, thank you. I will send a Mr Neville to collect it. Good-day!'

The November morning was still young when the errands were finished. It seemed a shame to waste the sunshine, so Gideon Masters persuaded her to return to Whitmore Square by way of Hyde Park. He entertained her so well with stories of India that she failed to notice when they made a second circuit.

Finally, the lieutenant fell silent and Alexa risked a glance at him—then turned quickly away, unable to meet those compelling, grey eyes.

'Are you really betrothed to Brunswick?' he said suddenly. 'Do I offer him congratulations?'

Bristling at his disapproving tone, she said

15

haughtily, 'It is usual, lieutenant, but in no way compulsory!'

'The engagement is official then?'

She clasped her hands tightly together inside her muff and looked away towards the mist-wreathed trees, their branches black against the milky sky.

'It will be announced in tomorrow's newspaper.'

'I see! May I ask when the wedding is to take place?'

'The date is not yet settled, but before Mr Brunswick returns to India.'

He was silent for along time, then he sighed. Speaking very gently, as though to a child, he said, 'You are so very young, Miss Alexandra Denton!'

She tossed her head in swift and defensive reaction. 'I am eighteen, lieutenant, almost nineteen. Perfectly old enough to know my own mind! Most girls my age are betrothed, and many already married!'

He nodded, a strand of dark hair falling across his brow in a way that inexplicably made her itch to smooth it back.

'The age-gap between you and Brunswick is quite a large one, particularly when taking into account the differences in experience.' He added gently, 'I feel that your upbringing has been very sheltered.'

She stared at the horse's ears, red flags of anger flying in her cheeks. How dare he say

16

such things to her on so short an acquaintance!

'I cannot see what possible business it is of yours, Lieutenant Masters,' she said coldly. 'It concerns only Mr Brunswick and myself!'

He sighed. 'That might have been true before today, Miss Denton, but when you walked through the parlour door, this morning, from that moment on, it became very much my business!'

She felt the sudden heat in her cheeks. 'You—you speak in riddles, lieutenant!'

His voice was warm, his smoky eyes caressing. 'I've waited a long time to meet you, Alexandra—twenty six years. Did you think I wouldn't know you when you came?'

Confused by his words, she didn't know how to answer. He was amusing himself by flirting with her, and although she had grown accustomed to young men flirting during the six months she had spent in London, this was like nothing she had ever experienced before. This man was like no other she had known.

'I don't understand you, lieutenant. You have no right to say such things. I am betrothed to the man I love. We shall marry in a few weeks time and I shall accompany him to India.'

Gideon Masters grew very still. He gazed with unseeing eyes at a box kite that jerked and fluttered like a crimson flame against the pale sky.

'I'm not sure that it's a good idea right now.

There's an undercurrent of unrest in northern India. Just a breath—a look in the eyes, a tone of voice. Nothing definite, nothing to put one's finger on. But it would be folly to ignore it.' He turned to look down at her and his eyes locked with hers. 'It would be wise to remain in London until things settle,' he concluded, but she had the feeling that he had left something unsaid.

She sat quietly for a moment, searching for the words to answer him. 'You are of the Queen's Regiments, lieutenant, while James, as you know, is a civil employee of the East India Company. He works for the governing officials and has close contact both with local dignitaries and with the officers commanding the sepoys, the native troops. If there was unrest among the populace, James would know of it. He's not in the least concerned for my safety—so I don't think it's your place to worry either! Or to tell me what is wise!'

Gideon Masters leaned towards her, so close she could smell his cologne, and her foolish heart began to pound. He touched her cheek with gentle fingers.

'Brunswick is a fool! Were you mine, I'd marry you today and carry you off to a place where no harm could ever come to you.'

'But I am not yours, lieutenant,' she said spiritedly. 'And after today, I don't expect ever to see you again.'

The shadows left his eyes and his chiselled

face melted into a whimsical smile that, despite everything, was very contagious. 'The gods wouldn't be so cruel, Alexandra! I may call you Alexandra?'

'Alexa,' she said faintly, fascinated by the cleft in his chin and wondering how it would feel if she were to trace it with her fingertip. Shocked by the thought, she straightened in her seat. 'Please, Lieutenant Masters, drive me home!'

'Then you won't elope with me, Alexa?'

The question was asked in so droll a manner that she knew, with relief, that he was teasing her again. Laughter bubbled in her throat, but to give voice to it would be her downfall, so she merely tossed her head and disdained to reply. He sighed audibly and clucking to the horse, turned its head in the direction of Whitmore Square.

'Good-day then, Alexa,' he said, his smoky eyes glowing as they smiled down into hers. 'I won't say goodbye. Despite your declaration, I'm sure we shall meet again! In the meantime, if I can be of any assistance please let me know. I'm at the Lawrence Club and expect to be there for the next week.'

The address came just in time to remind her, guiltily, of James and bite back the crazy impulse to invite the lieutenant to call upon her again. It was a temptation she must never succumb to! Things were going so right for her now. She was soon to marry her beloved James

19

and share his life in Meerut. She must not risk spoiling it all for the devastating attraction of a stranger.

'Goodbye,' she said determinedly. 'Thank you for your help.'

He clasped her offered hand warmly and bowed over it, raising it to his lips in the gesture he had used when they first met.

His bold, pirate's face was suddenly very serious as he said, 'Please reconsider your decision, Alexa! You shouldn't go to India just now—and Brunswick is too old for you; too worldly wise and set in his ways. I would make you a much better husband!'

Alexa snatched away her hand in fury. How dare this—this predator come so casually into her world and attempt to turn it upside down? Putting doubts in her mind. But there were no doubts! Her future was settled, her decision made, and it was so very right!

Her voice held a final note. 'Goodbye, lieutenant!'

Gideon Masters bowed again—bowed to the inevitable. Leaving her on the steps in the company of Neville, who had opened the door at the summons of the bell, he climbed back into the carriage without another word and with a smart salute, drove away.

And not before time, Alexa thought angrily, as she took her packages through to the drawing-room. She had been brought up on the Denton's estate in Norfolk where her only friends were those she had known since childhood, and although she had met several young men since coming to London, none had the devastating charm, the sheer masculine attraction, of the huge Lieutenant of Dragoons. Alexa knew that she was ill-equipped to deal with the Gideon Masters of this world, who made such cruel sport of her.

James did not arrive until after seven. Alexa met him in the hallway, concerned to see how tired he looked. He was unusually flustered and she guessed that his meeting at the Company offices hadn't gone well.

He made his apologies then bent and kissed her cheek. 'You received my message? I wasn't sure that Lieutenant Masters could be trusted to deliver it, but as he was passing close to Whitmore Square on his way to the country, I took the chance.'

She started. Gideon Masters, then, had been merely a messenger and had not been asked to take care of her. Alexa looked away so that James shouldn't see the spark of anger kindle in her eyes and wonder at the cause.

'I received your message, but I was hoping you would come sooner.'

'It was not from choice, dear girl, for I was delayed at the Company office. It has been a most difficult day—but I think perhaps it will be best if we discuss it with your parents.'

He sounded so serious that Alexa's heart filled with anxiety as she followed him into the

21

drawing-room where her parents were talking over a glass of wine.

'We were afraid you weren't coming,' Lady Emma said. 'Do sit down and join us.'

When Sir George had passed the decanter and James had poured port for himself and white wine for Alexa, he said gravely, 'I'm afraid I have received some unsettling news. I've been recalled. The Chief Official in Delhi has suffered a fatal heart attack and there's been a general re-shuffle. Things are in a mess and it's imperative that I return to take charge of the Company Office in Lucknow. I'll be working directly under Sir Henry Lawrence, the Chief Commissioner for Oudh.'

'But that's a promotion, my boy.' Sir George beamed. 'You couldn't work for a finer man. Pass the port—we must drink to this.'

'It's a long-awaited promotion,' James admitted, making no move towards the decanter. 'But badly timed for I am to sail from Tilbury on the twenty-third.'

There was a shocked silence broken by Alexa's dismayed, 'Oh, James, no!'

'But that's the day after tomorrow!' Lady Emma said faintly.

'Yes!' James stared unhappily into Alexa's worried eyes. Then, he took her hand and held it tightly in his own as he turned to Sir George. 'I realise that there's no time now for us to be married, sir, not in England. But if Alexa is willing, and you give your consent, she can sail with me and we will be married on the high seas.'

Sir George rose to his feet with an oath. 'My daughter, sir, will be married nowhere but in a consecrated church,' he snapped.

'Then we can be married immediately we arrive in Bombay. There are some fine churches there.'

There was a profound silence and the couple on the sofa looked anxiously at Sir George, but it was Lady Emma who declared, 'Unthinkable! My daughter's reputation would be compromised beyond saving and no breath of scandal has ever touched the Dentons. It's not possible for the two of you to travel aboard ship unmarried, as you must well realise, James—and even if It were, Alexa's dress cannot be made in time, and there is her trousseau to prepare! She simply cannot be ready by the twenty-third!'

James had expected no less. He took a deep breath as he rose to his feet in turn, and visibly squared his shoulders. 'Then will you give permission for Alexa to follow by a later ship?'

Again, it was Lady Emma who spoke for her husband seemed dumbfounded by the turn of events. 'It would not be seemly for a young girl to journey such a distance alone.'

'There will be several ladies travelling, the wives of officers and government officials,' James hastened to assure her. 'One of them will gladly act as companion and chaperon—it can be easily arranged.' He turned and smiled encouragement at Alexa. 'Someone trustworthy and congenial!'

'Oh, Papa, Mama—may I please?' Alexa begged, who could not bear the thought of waiting another five years for James to get his next home leave, of waiting another five years for India.

Lady Emma looked at her husband, her expression neutral now as she calmly awaited his decision. Sir George bent his head and brooded into the fire. Alexandra was young, inexperienced in affairs of the world, and too trusting, but James Brunswick was a sensible fellow who would take proper care of her.

'I don't see why not—if your mama agrees and things are properly arranged,' he said at last.

'Oh, Mama, please say yes,' Alexa pleaded.

Lady Emma smiled, her lovely face glowing in the firelight. 'It will be quite an adventure,' she offered.

Laughing with relief, Alexa flung delighted arms around James and hugged him, then ran to kiss her parents. 'Thank you, Papa—Mama!'

Neville appeared from nowhere with a tray of glasses and a magnum of champagne, and he was invited to propose a toast to the happy couple. Neville had paced the floor at Sir George's side until Alexa had uttered her first cry and the doctors had finally pronounced the mother safe.

'To Miss Alexa and Mr Brunswick, much happiness,' he cried.

'Alexa and James!'

Among much laughter, they toasted the proposed voyage—the coming nuptials—the couple's new life—James's promotion, and India.

The champagne swirled and bubbled in Alexa's mind. She was wildly happy, elated, almost light-headed for she—together with James, of course—was the centre of her parents' attention, an unaccustomed luxury for which she had waited all her young life. And here, at last, was the celebration she craved. Then, suddenly, without her quite knowing how it had happened, the party was over. She looked around in dismay.

James was talking politics with Sir George. Lady Emma had put down her glass and taken up her perpetual tapestry. The scene was a familiar, every-day one but, after the too-brief celebration, appeared totally unreal.

She caught Neville's eyes as he quietly left the room. Did she see doubt and anxiety in them? Despite the champagne and the warm fire, Alexa shivered.

James left an hour later and she went with him to the door. 'It's been a wonderful evening, Alexa,' he said contentedly. 'I'm sorry we won't be travelling out together, my dear, but I'll make sure you have a congenial companion.'

She looked up into his lean, handsome face, trying hard not to compare it with the dashing buccaneer attraction of the lieutenant who had come so boldly into her life and attempted to make her his prize. 'You'll come tomorrow, James?'

'Of course!' He took her shoulders and drew her against him. His lips were firm and warm upon hers. It was still not an entirely satisfactory kiss, but it was getting better. James, she felt sure, was a romantic at heart and she wished that he wouldn't hide his feelings quite so well. When they were married, she would encourage the warm side of his nature to blossom and they would be blissfully happy—as Mama and Papa were happy.

His voice when he spoke was intense. 'You will come out and marry me, Alexa?'

'Yes, James, of course I will!'

'Promise me faithfully!'

'I promise,' she said and again turned up her face to his.

This time his kiss was possessive. 'Remember,' he whispered, 'you belong to me!'

His smile was particularly warm as he said good-night and her heart sang. She was to be married to the man she loved; a man who loved her in return, and if their plans had to be altered, if she was forced to travel alone, it didn't matter. She would go at last to India!

CHAPTER THREE

The *Pride of Kent* sailed on the thirtieth of January, 1857. As the dark swell of water that divided ship from shore grew ever wider, Alexa leaned on the rail and waved again and again in the direction of the carriage in which Sir George and Lady Emma had taken refuge from the cold wind.

'Goodbye! Goodbye!'

As the land slipped away, Alexa knew she should feel greater sorrow at leaving her parents, but she was far too excited to feel anything but elation.

When the quay was no more than a smudge on the horizon, Alexa went below to the cabin adjoining that of Mrs Symonds, the wife of a surgeon major in Delhi, a seasoned traveller, and her chaperon and companion for the journey.

Mrs Symonds was the most imposing woman that Alexa had ever met. Tall and generously proportioned, of a regal bearing and stately gait, she quite overawed her fellow passengers.

Alexa had been similarly impressed when they were first introduced, but she had been privileged to glimpse the kindly, humorous soul hidden beneath the terrifying exterior.

The connecting doors were open. 'Do come

and have coffee, Alexandra,' Mrs Symonds called. 'You must be frozen after so long on deck.'

'I'm not cold at all,' Alexa assured her, but she was pleased to throw off her cloak and go through to Mrs Symonds' cabin that was so much larger and more comfortable than her own.

'Influence and intimidation, my dear,' her companion explained when asked how she had managed it, for the larger cabins were rare and avidly fought for.

Harriet Symonds passed a cup to Alexa. 'I think perhaps a little extra against the cold will not come amiss,' she said, producing a pretty, ceramic cologne bottle. She uncorked it and raised an eyebrow. 'Will you join me?'

Uncertain of the contents, Alexa refused, but she watched with interest as Mrs Symonds half-filled her own coffee cup, then topped it up with amber liquid from the bottle which smelled suspiciously like brandy.

Her chaperon caught Alexa's eye and smiled. 'Purely medicinal,' she confided in a whisper and were she anyone but the imposing Mrs Symonds, Alexa would have sworn her eyes twinkled. 'You must call me Harriet by the way, for I shall call you Alexandra!'

'Alexa, please!'

Harriet Symonds tutted disapprovingly, then drank with gusto from her cup. Her eyes were definitely twinkling now.

'Dinner, I'm told, is at seven o'clock sharp. We'll go in at seven-fifteen and make an entrance, so your best gown, Alexandra, and jewels. There are no titles on board, so we must establish our position as leading ladies from the first!'

Alexa lifted the hoops of her crinoline and sat down on Harriet's bed. Her eyes were dancing with amusement. 'I didn't know there were such beings aboard ship.'

'My dear child, there are always leading ladies!' Harriet drained her cup, poured another and added a dash from the cologne bottle. 'It's imperative if we want the captain's table, the most comfortable deckchairs, the most obliging steward, and the best food! It can go off considerably on the long stages,' she added darkly. 'We must lay claim from the start—and stand no nonsense!'

Alexa chuckled. Mrs Symonds, she was discovering, was not just awesome, but determined and devious. If such a long voyage could be fun, then Harriet would make it so!

So Alexa raided her trousseau and, wearing the beautifully-flounced, ivory lace-over-satin crinoline intended for her honeymoon, went resplendently into dinner in the company of Mrs Symonds, majestic in a purple gown and diamond tiara. The strategy proved successful and they were, thereafter, treated with the greatest deference.

'We shall derive as much enjoyment as

29

possible from this voyage, Alexandra,' Mrs Symonds told her later. 'The days will often prove tedious, the climate uncomfortable and the motion of the ship intolerable but, between times, we shall enjoy ourselves.'

To Alexa's great relief, after two wretched days in the Bay of Biscay, she proved a good sailor. There was plenty to do, for apart from long and delightful conversations with Harriet, walks on deck and various organised activities, she had brought a plentiful supply of books.

And if at night her dreams were persistently haunted by broad shoulders, a chiselled profile and smoke-grey eyes, she was able to banish them firmly throughout the daylight hours.

They finally reached journey's end on Sunday the seventeenth of March, 1857. They had been travelling for forty-six days!

To Alexa's eyes, the scene on the dock-side was one of utter chaos. Hordes of labourers swarmed over the quay and the ships like ants. The noise was deafening—particularly so after the comparative peace of the ocean. Strong, spicy smells rose to replace the now familiar scents of salt spray and tar. It was exotic, it was alien, it was enthralling! It was India, land of her birth and the place she had long dreamed of!

Leaning from the rail, Alexa drank in the scene before her. Her dark brown eyes searched the sea of humanity. There were several pale faces among the dark, and she scanned them carefully, looking for the one familiar face she longed to see. But though there were tall men and handsome men, James was not amongst them.

A hand touched her elbow. 'Come along, Alexandra,' Harriet cried. 'I've hired a bearer who will see to our luggage. Let's get away from this noise.'

'But James isn't here yet.'

'My dear, James will be at the hotel. We've docked hours early, and no-one waits unnecessarily in this blazing sun. How these ships manage to arrive in the right place on the right day amazes me, let alone at the right hour! Now, do come along!'

They said goodbye to the captain and his officers, and then Alexa followed her formidable companion down the gangplank and across the crowded quay to where canopied litters were waiting.

'This is Hakim!' Harriet said.

A sturdy Hindu with an intelligent, friendly face salaamed before assisting them into the doolies. The tough little coolies, four to each litter, took up their burdens and trotted away from the harbour and into the sweltering, teeming streets of Calcutta.

Alexa was never to fully recall details of that journey, only that she had never seen so much humanity packed into so confined a space. She had never heard such a babble of voices, or been assailed by such overpowering scents, as

31

there were in this exotic city swarming with humanity. By the time they reached the ornate frontage of the Imperial Hotel, Alexa felt exhausted.

To her relief, the interior of the hotel was calm and quiet and she went immediately to the desk to enquire after James.

'I'm sorry, Miss Denton,' the clerk said. 'Mr Brunswick has reserved a room, but he hasn't yet arrived. I will send word when he comes.'

The ladies signed the register and on Harriet's suggestion went out to the terrace overlooking the gardens, where palms and tinkling fountains lent a delicious coolness to the air.

'I told you we'd be in good time,' Harriet said, as they were ushered to a table. 'It's past noon, so we might as well have tiffin.'

They ordered chicken with saffron rice from one of the white-clad waiters, and Alexa was amused to see that Harriet had the same effect upon the hotel staff as she had upon everyone else, for the waiter went almost on the run to fill their order.

Furtively watching the other diners, who seemed totally at ease and somewhat bored, Alexa wondered if she would ever be so blasé or grow accustomed to the hit, and indifferent to the exotic surroundings.

'You'll soon become acclimatised, although no-one ever gets entirely used to the immense heat of the hot weather,' Harriet told her. 'In a month or so it will seem as if you've never lived anywhere else. So many Europeans remain out here after retirement, still calling Britain "home" until the day they die, but always putting off the departure date. India has a kind of magic that holds them and although it's often a love-hate relationship, they can't bear to leave her!'

Alexa looked off across the gardens, a little smile playing about her lips. She knew exactly what Harriet meant. The subcontinent had drawn her like a magnet for as long as she could remember.

Upstairs in her room, Alexa was delighted to find that her balcony overlooked the gardens. Her luggage was stacked neatly in one corner and, deciding not to wait for the maid whom she had shared throughout the voyage with Harriet, Alexa undressed and lay down beneath the muslin insect netting draped over the bed. She fell asleep almost immediately.

It was dusk when she woke. A young woman was moving quietly about the room, and Alexa saw that she had unpacked one of the trunks and was laying out fresh clothing.

Seeing that Alexa was awake, the woman put her hands together and bowed. Her face was round and smiling, and she had a caste mark between her brows. She was, Alexa guessed, about twenty years old.

'You must be the ayah Memsahib Symonds

33

promised to hire for me,' Alexa said, speaking in the Hindustani she had learned as a child and practised regularly with her parents. 'What is your name?'

'Seeta, Miss-sahiba!'

Seeta indicated with her hand and Alexa saw that she had prepared a bath. The water was cool, perfumed and very refreshing. Seeta helped her dress and Alexa found that she had laid out exactly the right clothing. The ayah was efficient and agreeable and Alexa took an immediate liking to her.

'Have you family in Calcutta, Seeta?'

'Not now, Miss-sahiba. Both my parents are dead.'

'Then will you come with me to Lucknow?'

The ayah put her hands together and bowed. 'I wish it very much,' she said with a wide smile.

There was no news of James at the desk and Alexa spent a somewhat worried evening despite Harriet's attempts to cheer her.

'This is a vast country, my dear. Things can so easily go wrong. Flash floods wash away roads, horses go lame, servants lose baggage . . . so many things!'

Alexa wasn't entirely comforted. He'd had months to prepare for her arrival, and early docking or not, he should be here to meet her. Unless something was horribly wrong . . .

'There'll be a perfectly logical explanation. Nothing travels faster than bad news,' Harriet

34

said firmly. 'I'd rather hoped that Jonathan would be here, but obviously his duties have prevented it. But he'll come to Lucknow, I'm sure, and in the meantime, I'm not going to worry myself grey that he's been kidnapped by a lecherous maharani or trampled by elephants—and neither should you!'

Alexa giggled, then had the grace to blush. Harriet was such a seasoned traveller, so confident and sure, that it was easy to forget that she was longing to see her husband equally as much as Alexa longed to see James.

'Harriet, I'm sorry! I've been a bear all evening, and it's harder for you! You must be quite desperate to get me off your hands after all these weeks!'

'Nonsense! I've enjoyed your company immensely and will be loath to part with you!' Harriet speared a square of curried beef and peered at Alexa over the top of it. 'The females at Delhi are a droopy lot on the whole, and for some reason quite terrified of me.'

Alexa's dark eyes twinkled into Harriet's hazel ones. 'I can't imagine why,' she said, and they collapsed in laughter.

Laughter had the desired effect and Alexa stopped worrying about James. She slept soundly and woke very early. The hotel was quiet, and guests seemed still to be sleeping, but no sooner had she risen from her bed than Seeta appeared, bowing and smiling and wishing her good-morning. The girl was a treasure and Alexa was pleased to have her.

Downstairs, she crossed immediately to the desk.

'This has just arrived, madam,' the clerk said, offering a buff envelope. It contained a message telegraphed to Government House and sent over to the hotel. James had been laid low with a recurrence of a fever he had contracted years before in East Africa.

His message concluded . . . *recovering but unable to meet in time. Please remain with Mrs Symonds until Lucknow. Impatiently awaiting your arrival. Devotedly, James.*

Alexa crumpled the form, thrust it into her pocket and went through to the terrace where breakfast was being served. She took scrambled eggs and coffee, eating mechanically, torn between relief that James was safe and a deep disappointment that he couldn't meet her, that they wouldn't travel together across the wide horizons of India.

She had intended to go with James to the bazaar and buy a present for Harriet to thank her for all her kindnesses and for the companionship that had made the voyage so pleasant. In James's absence, Alexa saw no reason why she shouldn't buy the gift herself. She had plentiful funds and four hours before they were due to leave Calcutta.

Knowing that Harriet wouldn't make an appearance for at least another hour, Alexa went to the reception desk and requested

36

paper and pen. She wrote a note to her friend and left it with the clerk. Then she sent a bell-boy to fetch a hat and a parasol from her room and went out into the bustling morning.

Alexa asked the doorman to summon a doolie. He seemed reluctant but when she insisted, flicked his fingers and a litter appeared like magic. She instructed the coolies to carry her to the bazaar of the silversmiths.

Shopkeepers were raising their shutters preparing for the first customers of the day. Sweepers were busy whisking clean the streets. Beggars were emerging from the alleyways. People were already about their business for the day started early before the great heat of the afternoon.

Alexa paid off the coolies at the entrance to the bazaar and set out to investigate. She was instantly besieged by peddlers selling cheap trinkets, and by children clamouring for baksheesh. Alexa threw a handful of small coins and, as they scrambled to retrieve them, escaped into one of the shops.

The silversmith produced many items for her inspection, the superb workmanship of which entranced her. She selected a beautifully-engraved stud box for James, but was unable to decide on a gift for Harriet. There was a fine hip flask that she longed to buy, but she knew that Harriet preferred the anonymity of the cologne bottle.

Alexa wandered on down the street, finding

37

new delights along the way. There were many beautiful things to tempt her but, undecided, she ventured farther, her enjoyment spoiled only by the persistent pestering of the retinue of beggars that refused to leave her.

Hoping to lose them, she turned into another alleyway and found herself outside a shop selling the most intricate jade carvings. Joyfully, she browsed, amazed at the artistry, scarcely aware of time passing and eventually found an enchanting jade figurine of a goddess of Junoesque proportions which she was sure Harriet would appreciate.

The asking price was exorbitant, but she knew to haggle and they eventually settled on a figure satisfactory to both shopkeeper and customer.

Out in the street again with the gift safely in her reticule, she was approached by an old crone, fragile and bent and hung about with rags. The woman's face was like wrinkled parchment and there was such patient suffering in the milky depths of her eyes that Alexa's heart was wrung with compassion.

Silently, pleadingly, the beggar extended a skeleton hand as frail as a dried leaf, and Alexa fumbled in her purse and gently pressed two rupees into it. Silently, the woman's lips moved as she seemed to crumble away into the shadows.

Immediately, Alexa was pounced upon by a hoard of ragged men. No pleading beggars these, but ruffians who shouted aggressively in their native tongues demanding alms. These were of a different ilk to the old woman and to the children in the bazaar. These were scoundrels and hooligans. There was an open threat in their demands and hatred in the faces. They pressed closely about her, hemming her in.

Alexa was instantly aware of the danger! Alarm set her heart thudding but she faced them bravely.

'Let me through,' she cried with all the authority she could muster. 'Let me through—make way!' But her voice was lost in the general clamour.

Knowing that she would find no help here in the alley, she tried to push towards the main street. The mob about her grew angrier. They formed an almost solid barricade, so that she made little headway. Hands strived to detain her, clutched at her gown, tried to pull the reticule out of her grasp.

Her heart was hammering with fright and panic rose in a thick tide in her throat. 'Make way! Please make way,' she cried again but still the men pressed about her, insolently jeering, roughly touching. She felt her muslin dress rip. Suddenly, terror gave her strength.

Clutching the handles of her reticule tightly, she screamed at them and lashed out with it, using the heavy statuette inside as a weapon. Several telling blows landed, the solid thump as they connected jarring her arm. Then the reticule was grabbed and held. She hung on to it, wrestling frantically with a wild-eyed fellow who seemed to be the ring-leader. He twisted the bag in her grip and she felt the skin on her hands tear. Despairingly, she opened her mouth and screamed defiance at the top of her lungs.

It seemed to have a galvanising effect. The ruffian rose into the air and crashed backwards. Alexa heard the dull thud of fists on flesh and another man followed the first. There was a commotion of movement, of shouting, of blows. Several more of the scoundrels went crashing into the surrounding walls. The rest fled from her like shadows before the sun. There was a wild tattoo of running feet that rapidly faded into silence.

Alexa was left facing a bright blue expanse that filled her vision. Her bewildered eyes followed a double line of military buttons upward and she looked into a fearsome, buccaneer face. A pair of smoky-grey eyes smouldered with the light of battle.

'Oh, Alexa,' Gideon Masters said, his deep voice reproachful. 'A lone woman with money in her purse should never frequent back alleys.'

Involuntarily, she clutched his sleeve and stared up at him as though afraid he might vanish. 'I was only buying a gift. I thought it would be all right!'

40

'Normally it would. Even those ruffians were never so bold as to harm a lady. But strange things are happening at the moment.' He looked down at her stricken face and said very gently, 'You must remember that there is real poverty here and it is a great temptation when money is flashed around.'

'But I only gave the poor woman two rupees,' she protested spiritedly, angry that he should blame her for the ruffians' behaviour. Then, suddenly, to her great horror, tears welled into her eyes and trembled on her lashes. 'Oh, lieutenant,' she whispered broken-heartedly. 'The poor woman was so incredibly thin and frail—so incredibly old!'

He sighed and his voice was infinitely tender. 'I know!' And he cradled her in his arms as she laid her head against the comforting expanse of his blue uniform jacket and wept.

CHAPTER FOUR

The Grand Trunk Road was the main artery of British India, linking Calcutta to distant Peshawar in the western Punjab. Along its sun-baked length travelled an endless stream of vehicles.

From the bullock cart in which she rode, Alexa never tired of watching the great elephants, their howdahs packed with officers returning from leave, the carts, doolies, rickshaws, carriages, camels and bicycles that formed an ever-moving two-way stream along the great highway.

She shared the cart with Harriet and Mrs Homes, the wife of a colonel stationed at Cawnpore. At the outset, Mrs Homes produced a pack of cards.

'Will you play, Miss Denton? It passes the time most pleasantly.'

'Thank you, but I'm far too distracted to concentrate,' Alexa said waving to a group of children who stood at the roadside. 'It's all so new and exciting.'

When they couldn't change her mind, the two matrons engaged in endless games of gin rummy using a board balanced across their laps, for their wide skirts left no room for even the smallest camp table.

A novel lay unopened at Alexa's side for it

was impossible to read with so much happening. The high-spirited officers frequently ran camel races over the flat land bordering the road, and sometimes foot races, the participants sweating and gasping alarmingly in the heat.

There were villages and towns to see, wayside shrines, mosques and temples. Alexa drank in the scenes with delight, feeling that she had at last come home.

Each noon, when the sun was at its zenith, a general halt was called. Tents were erected along the verges. The busy road was suddenly deserted as the travellers sought refuge from the terrible heat. At five o'clock, the processions resumed until it grew too dark to travel. Then the tents were erected once more and cooking fires winked along the fifteen hundred miles of road. It was in the evenings that Lieutenant Masters joined Alexa and Harriet in their encampment.

Alexa often caught glimpses of him during the day on his big, white horse, riding parallel to the road at the head of a platoon of soldiers.

'There was a spot of bother in Barrackpore,' he'd told her when she'd asked how he came to be in Calcutta. 'It was soon settled, but I had dispatches to deliver at Government House before I could take my men back to Rawalpindi.'

'Fortunately for me,' she'd admitted.

One afternoon, when the bullock cart was halted so that a broken shaft could be mended,

43

Alexa noticed a pin-prick of light flashing from the shoulder of a hill. From the shade of her parasol, she watched Lieutenant Masters despatch three of his men while he studied the area through a field glass. The flickering eventually stopped and a little later, the troopers returned.

When Gideon rode over to see how the repair was progressing, Alexa called to him. 'What caused those flashes of light, Lieutenant Masters? May I look?'

'These are military equipment, Alexa,' he said in mock horror. 'I'd be court-marshalled for allowing them into the hands of a civilian— even such pretty hands as yours!'

'I won't tell, if you don't,' Alexa retorted with an impatient toss of her head.

'It was no more than sunlight flashing on a waterfall,' he told her lightly, his smoke-grey eyes laughing at her annoyance.

He spoke in rapid Hindustani to the driver and having received an assurance that the repair was almost completed, galloped away leaving Alexa to stare thoughtfully at the hills.

'Probably a discontent, dear,' Mrs Homes said.

'What do you mean, a discontent?' Harriet demanded.

'Something my husband mentioned in his last letter. Seems there's some unrest among the populace. Harold thinks it has something to do with religion, with Shiva.'

Alexa had heard of Shiva, the great god who was said to dwell in the distant Himalayas. She looked across at Harriet and saw that she was frowning.

'Exactly what did Harold say?' Harriet asked.

'It was told to him by his Indian captain. He said that out of the east, the great god Shiva is sending messages across the earth threatening fire, justice and punishment. And that's all the fellow would say. Harold thinks it's one of those insane, hot-weather things that crop up from time to time.'

Harriet made a sound like an engine releasing steam. 'Very likely, and it will no doubt die a natural death once the monsoons come.'

The matrons went back to their game and Alexa looked out across the landscape to where a troop of distant riders kept station. She hated to admit it, but she was glad that Gideon Masters was nearby.

During the first of his evening visits, the lieutenant, who was already acquainted with the Symonds, told Harriet that he and Alexa were friends.

'We met at her home in Whitmore Square,' he said artlessly.

The heat and discomfort of the unsprung cart had considerably sapped Harriet's strength or she would not have fallen for so blatant a ploy. As it was, believing that the two

45

young people were well acquainted, she had little compunction about retiring early and leaving them to entertain each other.

Alexa was guiltily aware that she should correct the impression, but somehow the words remained unspoken.

'There's something timeless about this journey,' she said one night when they were settled in their camp chairs within sound, if not sight, of her chaperon's tent. 'It seems as if we'll go on for ever and never reach Lucknow.'

'We'll reach it all too soon!' he said glumly. 'I'm usually impatient to return to my regiment, but that was before I met you again, Alexa. Before I knew that another man is waiting to claim you. Now I hope we'll never arrive. Is there nothing I can do to stop you marrying James Brunswick?'

She couldn't see his face in the darkness, but his chiselled profile was clearly etched against the star-hung sky. She had no way of knowing whether he was serious or merely teasing.

She said, as firmly as she could, 'Marriage to James is the only reason that I've travelled such a distance.'

'Is it, Alexa? Are you sure? Was it not also because of your great desire to return to India? Didn't James present the way and the means?'

She sensed his eyes upon her and was glad that the darkness hid the hot flush that rose to her face. 'Of course not,' she said sharply. 'What a horrid thing to say.'

He continued to look at her, but when he spoke again it was a complete change of subject.

'Have you ever seen the Ganges, Alexa?'

'The holy river?'

'It is said that its flow is as strong and unchanging as life itself. For Hindus it is indeed a holy river.' He leaned forward in his chair, his dark bulk shutting out the stars. 'Tomorrow evening, we will be near Benares and within reach of the Ganges. I shall take you to visit it.'

'But won't it be dark?'

His voice was firm. 'There'll be a full moon and the stars will light the water for us. It's the best way to see the Ganges.' He reached out and his fingers lightly touched her forearm. 'You can't be in India, Alexa, and not see the Ganges by moonlight!'

She hesitated, aware that her heart was racing. To be alone in the moonlight with Gideon Masters was foolish, begging trouble. But was there really any harm? The lieutenant was a gentleman and wouldn't take advantage of her.

Before she could decide, Harriet's voice carried from the dark interior of the tent. 'It's time to retire, Alexandra. We've an early start, remember.'

Gideon rose immediately. 'I'll say good-night, and look forward to tomorrow evening.' Hs raised her hand, not to his lips as he usually did, but laid it momentarily against his cheek. Then he turned towards the dark bulk of the tents. 'Good-night, Harriet! Pleasant dreams!'

* * *

Woken early by the noisy bustle of pre-dawn preparations, Alexa vowed that never again would she sit alone with Lieutenant Masters. But when Gideon arrived that evening with two horses, and sweetmeats with which to charm Harriet, Alexa found herself changing into an emerald-green riding habit and allowing him to lift her to the saddle.

The night was dark but the rising moon lit the track before them. As they rode, Alexa's shyness receded. Excitement loosened her tongue and she chatted happily, more at ease with her companion than she had ever been before. Gideon responded to her mood and it was a carefree couple who cantered northward.

When at last they topped a small rise, they saw below them the dark silhouette of trees. Beyond was the glittering sheen of the Ganges as it unrolled its silken length across the silent countryside.

Reining in among the trees, Gideon lifted her down. 'We'll walk from here and leave the horses to rest,' he said, taking her hand.

48

The river was as promised, a wide expanse of strong-flowing water reflecting a myriad stars, the full moon laying a shimmering path of light across its surface. Standing there on the bank, Alexa felt the enduring might of the holy river.

'Oh, Gideon,' she said softly, using his Christian name for the first time. 'It's beautiful—so cool and tranquil!' She tilted her head. 'Listen!'

Somewhere in the distance a drum began to throb. It was joined by a sitar, the singing notes of the music haunting, but perfectly in tune with the night.

'There's a village across the water. If you look between the trees, you can just see the lights of their fires far out on the plain.'

'It looks very lonely—so isolated, so far away from everything.'

'It wouldn't suit a city-dweller like you,' he teased, 'but the villagers are a contented lot. The land here is well-irrigated and productive, and far enough from the delta to escape the worst of the annual floods.'

They turned and walked along a rough pathway beside the river, barely definable in the darkness. Alexa stumbled and Gideon took her arm and wound it through his and she was content to leave it there.

She looked up at him, a tall silhouette in the moonlight. 'I hear the orchards of Kent in your voice, Gideon, but do I also detect a touch of

49

the north country?'

'You've found me out, Alexa! I was born in Berwick-on-Tweed, and my grandparents still live there. But my parents moved to Rochester when I—'

He broke off suddenly, clutched her shoulders and flung her bodily to the ground. Her shocked cry was short-lived as she heard the dull thud of a missile striking the tree above her head and the loud report of a rifle shot. There was another, lighter report from beside her, an oath in Hindi, and the ground vibrated to the thud of bare feet running.

'Stay down,' Gideon snapped.

Then, Alexa was alone, listening to the sound of his booted feet racing in pursuit. They faded into the distance and for a long time there was a heavy silence broken only by the lap of the river against the bank.

Her heart was thudding uncomfortably against her ribs as she strained for sounds in the night. Where was Gideon? What was happening out there in the darkness? The attacker had a rifle and could easily lie in ambush. Gideon had fired the pistol shot, so he was armed, but he was still in danger.

From somewhere far off came another pistol shot, followed almost immediately by a heavier report. Alexa scrambled to her feet. She had to find Gideon! He could be hurt, lying in the dirt somewhere. But where? Which way? The moon had vanished behind cloud, and the thick darkness disorientated her. She took several steps along what she thought was the path and felt the bank crumble. For one awful moment she tottered over a drop, saw the gleam of water below, and flung herself backward just as her feet began to slide. She had almost walked into the river.

Turning about, she edged cautiously forward but, before she had gone many yards, her feet snagged in a tree root and she stumbled. The ground underfoot was stony now. She had completely lost the path and she stopped again, defeated by the darkness.

There were no further gunshots. But she had to find Gideon. He could be lying wounded somewhere. She shivered with fear and, dropping to her knees, crawled forward, searching for the pathway with her out-stretched hands.

Suddenly, the silence was broken by the flick of a dislodged stone and the soft splash as it rolled into the water. Her heart lurched in her chest as a giant shadow loomed towards her.

'Gideon?' she whispered fearfully, 'Gideon, is it you?'

'It's all right, my darling!' And suddenly he was there, big and strong and solid and safe, lifting her with ease, and she was in his arms, clinging tightly as he kissed her brow, her cheek, her lips.

They clung together in the thick, hot

51

darkness there beside the Ganges while the stars wheeled above them and the capricious moon forsook her hiding place to bathe them in light, lost to everything but each other.

How long it was before Alexa regained her senses, she never knew. But the moon was well down when she suddenly realised that this was complete and utter folly. She was betrothed to James. He trusted her, and even now was making arrangements for their wedding. Was she so fickle that she could allow the recent danger to blind her to all else but the attraction of Gideon Masters?

With a cry, she wrenched herself from his arms and struggled free. Stepping back, she held up a fending hand as he made to embrace her again.

'Please—take me back to the encampment,' she whispered, oblivious of the tears shining in her eyes. 'We must go back. Harriet may be worrying.'

Gideon was obviously puzzled, but accepted her request without question.

'Of course, my darling,' he said with a glance at the sky, 'I've kept you too long. Dawn isn't far away. Take my arm.'

Although stricken with guilt, she was glad to lean upon him as they retraced their steps. By unspoken consent, they stood a few moments looking out over the water, impressing its image upon their memories. Then, they turned their backs upon the holy river and walked up through the trees to their horses.

As they rode back through the sleeping countryside, Alexa was aware of his puzzled glances. To break the awkward silence, she asked lightly, 'Who was the gunman? Why did he wish to injure total strangers? If you hadn't reacted so swiftly, we might have been killed.'

'There were three of them, armed robbers, travelling the river path. I believe they came upon us by accident and sought to rob us of whatever we carried. Fortunately, only one had a rifle and that is now rusting on the bottom of the river. They got away I'm afraid, but one will have a very sore head in the morning, and another should be carrying my pistol ball in his shoulder. I'll get the Subahdar-Major in Benares to send some sepoys over in the morning and see what they can discover,' he concluded.

Alexa was silent, sensing that he was more concerned about the surprise attack than he wanted her to know. She had the sudden impulse to question him further, but fearing that he wouldn't answer, held silent.

'I hope it hasn't completely ruined the outing for you, Alexa,' he said anxiously. 'For me, it was a most wonderful night, one I shall always remember.'

'I fear we stayed too long—but I, too, will not forget the Ganges.'

They spoke little after that. Alexa was aware of his eyes upon her, but she looked resolutely ahead for to look at him was to weaken, and if she weakened, she was lost.

All was quiet at the encampment. The fire was low as the watchman slept in his blanket beside it, and Gideon cast him a frowning glance before he lifted Alexa from the saddle.

'I'll see you this evening, my darling,' he told her with a glance to where dawn tinted the eastern sky. His eyes glowed as he looked at her. 'I can't bear to leave you! I'll count the minutes and wish them gone!'

He made to embrace her but she stepped back almost in panic. Anguish lent an angry edge to her voice. 'Please, don't! You mustn't come again. This evening was a mistake. The darkness, the danger . . . I was afraid for you! I acted impulsively and never intended you to think . . . I'm pledged to James.' When he didn't reply, she said desperately, 'James is waiting for me. Everything is arranged. My parents expect us to marry—'

He interrupted her, crying incredulously, 'After the way you returned my kisses, I can't believe what you are saying! Surely you aren't still intent upon this marriage with Brunswick? When you so obviously don't love him?'

'But I do, I do!'

'You do no-one a service by professing a love you don't feel, Alexa. You can't be so foolish!'

Stung by his scorn, she lifted her chin. 'You have no right to speak to me like that,

54

lieutenant. I may have lost my head a moment, forgotten myself, but that doesn't mean that I don't love James. We'll be very happy—'

With an angry exclamation, he reached for her, his mouth stopping her words. His kiss was hard, almost brutal. Then he put her from him and shook her until tears jerked from her eyes. 'You little idiot, Alexa! Oh, you foolish, stubborn, loyal, little idiot! Life's too short for games!'

'Go! Please go!' she cried almost hysterically.

The anger left him. His voice filled with sadness. 'Very well, if that's what you really want. If you are sure your happiness lies with Brunswick, so be it.'

He released her so abruptly that she staggered and almost fell, but he had turned on his heel and with a sharp word to the sleepy watchman that brought the fellow smartly to attention strode away . . .

Alexa lay on her cot and watched the dawn light creep into the tent and her heart was as desolate as the dusty road they travelled—the road that was leading her to marriage with James. To her horror, she could barely remember how he looked. She closed her eyes conjuring his image, but it was the adored face of her papa which rose in her mind and the panic returned, threatening to engulf her.

She remembered that in London she had loved James, and when she saw him, she would surely love him again. It was just that the moon and the river had got in the way—India had got in the way.

If James had met her in Calcutta, she wouldn't have succumbed to smoky eyes, a bold profile and a deep, laughing voice. When she and James met again, this unfortunate episode would be forgotten. Gideon would be forgotten.

*   *   *

The days passed and the lieutenant heeded Alexa's words. He neither approached the bullock cart, nor came to their encampment.

Harriet Symonds regretted Gideon's absence and probed sharply, but receiving only evasive replies, finally desisted. She was fond of both Alexandra and Gideon, and guessed far more than either young person imagined, and she was deeply disturbed. But she had given her word to Alexandra's father, and she also had a duty to James Brunswick in the matter. Deciding that it was best to let sleeping dogs lie, she accepted the situation.

From time to time, Alexa saw Gideon with his men riding out on the plain, but he didn't turn his head to seek her out as he had previously done. It was as if she no longer existed—that the evening by the Ganges had never been.

That is how I want it, she thought stoutly.

And if she missed him terribly, it was only to be expected for there was little enough diversion now that the novelty of the journey had waned. And if she felt absolutely wretched, it was the heat and the jolting and the tedium that made her so.

It was seven hundred miles from Calcutta to Lucknow and progress in the bullock cart was slow, but the day came when they reached Cawnpore, and saying goodbye to Mrs Homes, turned off the Grand Trunk Road on to a lesser road leading northward. Instead of Delhi, Lahore and Peshawar, the signposts now read Lucknow and Sitapore. They were nearing journey's end.

When they entered the bustling city of Lucknow, Alexa saw Gideon Masters among them and, perversely, found his presence comforting for now that her reunion with James was imminent, she was strangely apprehensive.

But her nerves were forgotten as the cart wound its way through the city, passing slender towers, palaces and domes, until they came to the imposing Residency, home of the Chief Commissioner, which overlooked the city.

The Residency courtyard was a meeting place for both civilians and military. On the wide verandas, the populace took tea and watched for the arrival of friends and relatives. Military stations were small worlds and outside news was avidly sought—particularly news from England.

There were many friends of Harriet's in the courtyard and they fell upon her with cries of delight and she and Alexa were borne off to the shady verandas.

Alexa tried to win free for she was afraid of missing James among so many. But she was not allowed to escape! The newcomers were kept busy answering questions on fashions, and the latest society scandals. Alexa, as a soon-to-be bride, came in for particular attention as they demanded details of her dress and trousseau as well as her life history.

Alexa answered as best she could while her eyes watched the courtyard, and suddenly she saw him, striding up past the banqueting hall that adjoined the Residency, tall and slender, immaculately groomed and handsome, looking just as he had when she had waved him goodbye at Tilbury four months earlier.

Her heart gave a great thump of relief. She had been so afraid that she wouldn't recognise him, for there had been times when she couldn't recall his image. The sepia photograph he had given her in London was indistinct and faded showing the wooden, formal image of a stranger. But she knew him at once! Apart from a deeper tan, James hadn't changed at all.

His eyes had found her almost immediately. He smiled and waved and shouted her name above the hubbub.

'Alexa! Alexa!'

'James!' With a glad cry, she lifted her skirts, pushed through the crowd that surrounded her, and ran across the courtyard to meet him.

CHAPTER FIVE

'Do have some tea,' Reverend Anderson said. They were seated on the veranda of the Rectory, a building adjacent to the Residency.

The reverend, known throughout the community as 'Padre,' smiled at Alexa, his dark eyes gleaming.

'I wonder if you realise, Miss Denton, what excitement your coming has generated in our small community? Regrettably, we are rather a closed world. A newcomer in our midst is always most welcome.'

His happy smile widened, encompassing James. 'And what a delight to be asked to officiate at a wedding! My work, alas, involves far more funerals than weddings—particularly after the cholera outbreak last year. In fact, I do believe this will be only the third wedding in eighteen months. But don't worry, I shall refresh my memory as to the order of service and everything will be perfection on the day. If you will remind me of the actual date, Mr Brunswick?'

'The twenty-eighth, Padre!'

The priest rifled busily through his parish diary. 'Yes, here we are! Nine thirty, marriage of James Albert Brunswick to Alexandra Jane Denton. I have it pencilled in!' He beamed happily from one to the other as if expecting applause. 'We would like an organist and a choir, Padre, and bells, if possible,' Alexa said a little anxiously, for the little rector did seem somewhat disorganised.

'Bells you shall have, Miss Denton—or rather bell for we have just the one, but I have arranged with my colleagues in the other churches to ring their bells as soon as ours is heard, so the whole city will resound with the news of your union. Mr Clamp is the organist, although the organ is sadly in need of an overhaul—the humidity plays havoc with the bellows and the pipes, you know.' He brightened. 'But there are some fine voices among the 32nd Foot who will be happy to earn a rupee or two.'

'You seem to have everything well in hand, Padre,' James said, and Alexa nodded agreement. So why didn't she feel happy? Why did she feel so trapped?

'You've chosen the hymns, I take it?' the padre asked and, when Alexa listed them he enthused. 'An excellent choice!'

Oblivious to James's frown, he added hospitably, 'You've time for a noggin, I'm sure.' His plump hand motioned to a wine table near his visitor's elbow. 'Help yourself, Mr Brunswick. Can we tempt you, Miss Denton?'

'Tea is fine, thank you, Padre.'

James, who had half-filled two tumblers with whisky, handed one to his host and downed the other in three noisy swallows. Putting down the glass, he looked ostentatiously at his pocket watch. 'If that's all, Padre?'

'Nearly done!' The priest rummaged through a battered leather folder. 'We seem to have all the paperwork, licence, declaration. We need Miss Denton's birth certificate, of course, and a form of consent from her legal guardian, but otherwise—'

Alexa produced the documents and he perused them carefully.

'Female, Alexandra Jane . . . twenty-seventh June, 1838, Simla.' He looked up with a smile. 'A native, I see, ha, ha!' He scanned the remaining paper. 'Consent to the marriage of my daughter . . . to Mr James Albert . . . Christian rites . . . Protestant church at Lucknow, Oudh, northern India. Signed, Sir James Denton, father, Whitmore Square, London. Good these are quite in order.'

'Then everything's arranged!' James was already on his feet.

'Just a date for the rehearsal,' the padre hastened to say as the prospective groom grasped his future bride by the elbow, raised her to her feet, and edged her nearer to the steps. 'Shall we say, Monday, the twenty-seventh, at five?'

'I really don't think—'

'The twenty-seventh at five will be fine, thank you, Padre,' Alexa replied.

They said their goodbyes, and as they walked across the courtyard, Alexa scolded, 'You were quite rude to Reverend Anderson, James. He's a nice man and has obviously gone to enormous trouble on our behalf.'

'He's a boring old wind-bag,' he retorted. 'I've no time for such.' His voice softened as he smiled down at her. 'We have far nicer things to do—and dinner is but one of them!'

He laughed delightedly as Alexa inexplicably blushed, and was furious at herself for doing so.

Brigadier General Sir Henry Lawrence had invited Alexa and Harriet to stay at the residency until the wedding. Sir Henry, Chief Commissioner for Oudh, was visiting Sitapore on official duty, and as they were the only guests at that time, the servants had prepared the small supper room.

They found Harriet in an ante-room talking to a middle-aged man, round-shouldered, grey-haired, whose skin had yellowed with sun and fever. But his eyes were alert and kindly, and he looked up with a smile as the couple came in.

'Alexandra, my dear, come and meet Jonathan! He and James have already met.' Harriet's eyes were bright as a young girl's, and when she looked at her husband, the love shone blatantly from her face.

'I'm delighted to meet you, Major. I've heard so much about you and suffered such guilt at keeping Harriet from you when she's been so long away. It's quite dreadful that you had to come all this way to fetch her. I know she's longing to return home to Delhi. But she insists upon staying for the wedding and nothing I say will persuade her otherwise.'

Jonathan laughed and his face came suddenly alive so that Alexa realised with surprise that he was a very attractive man.

'My dear Miss Denton, nothing and no-one can move Harriet when she's made up her mind. I've long since stopped trying. But it has given me the opportunity to meet you sooner than would otherwise be possible—and to be perfectly frank, I'm looking forward to this wedding as much as she is. James is a very lucky man.' He leaned towards her, his pale eyes twinkled. 'I know I'm asking the impossible, but the reception . . . I live in hope that one day, there'll be smoked salmon on the menu, and English, honey-cured ham.'

'Will you never stop thinking of your stomach, Jonathan?' his wife scolded. 'It isn't fair! I eat like a bird,' she said virtuously and falsely. 'And look at the size of me. Whereas you are a positive glutton and are nothing but skin and bone. And do call her Alexa. She is, after all, to be a frequent visitor to our house!'

'A delightful prospect—but only if she calls me Jonathan.'

The supper room was hot and stuffy for the Brigadier General had ordered several of the lower windows to be bricked up. 'For security reasons,' his secretary had told the women when they asked—and James had just shrugged the matter off.

'The old man's over-cautious. There's been a few hiccups with the new cartridges,' he confided. 'But the sepoys will come to them given time. They're the best soldiers in the world, but superstitious. Been spooked by this Shiva business. No-one's talking, but there's something afoot. It's a mystery difficult for the European mind to get to grips with, but it will all fizzle out when the monsoons come. Nothing for the Chief Commissioner to get windy about.'

The bricked-up windows made the lower floors stiflingly hot, however, despite the sweeping fans and the straw matting hung upon the walls and kept constantly damp by the water carriers. As soon as dinner was over, the four sought refuge in the garden.

James and Jonathan were soon discussing the forthcoming polo match against the Rajah of Kipore and they were shortly joined by Hugh Waldicott, James's colleague and chosen groom's-man. Hugh's wife, Jenny, whose ten-year-old twin daughters had been earmarked as bridesmaids, turned out to be a rather delicate-looking woman of faded prettiness.

'Have you a preference for colour, Miss Denton?' she asked anxiously. 'Only James insists that pink is your favourite and the girls have quite vivid titian hair.'

Alexa shook her head. 'I adore pink roses, but otherwise have no preference. I have with me a bolt of very pretty white muslin sprigged with forget-me-nots that I hope will be suitable for your daughters.'

Mrs Waldicott's relief was obvious. 'It sounds delightful. I had awful visions of my poor carrot-tops following you down the aisle like a pair of peeled shrimps. Oh, you mustn't laugh, Mrs Symonds. It would have been an utter disaster . . .' But she couldn't continue and joined her companions who, like schoolgirls, were convulsed in a fit of giggles.

'I'm glad that's settled,' Alexa declared, when she could speak. 'What are your daughter's names Mrs Waldicott?'

'Faith and Hope.' She touched the bulge only just perceptible beneath the voluminous folds of her skirt. 'And in a month, we might well have a Charity.'

'You are going to the hills for the confinement, of course,' Harriet said, and it was almost a command.

'Well—I hadn't intended. Hugh has so much work—'

'Immediately after the wedding, take the girls and go,' Harriet said flatly. 'Hang the expense! I'll ask Jonathan to have a word with your husband. It's not wise to stay in Lucknow when you'll be more—more comfortable in the hills.'

66

Jenny Waldicott nodded noncommittally, while Alexa wondered what her astute friend had really wanted to say.

When the Waldicotts left, the four walked together up the stone staircases to the second floor where the guest rooms were located. They stopped for a moment in the recessed bay of a wide, latticed window. The night breeze had come at last and its hot breath whispered through the galleries.

'Would you like my rented carriage tomorrow, Alexa?' Jonathan Symonds said. 'Harriet tells me that you've been inundated with invitations from the ladies. I thought you might like to make use of it.'

'That's very kind! I have a full schedule beginning with coffee at ten, and ending with tea at Mrs Bennett's at five. They say the Bennett bungalow is really beautiful. When am I to see your—our bungalow, James?'

'Not quite yet, my dear,' he hastened to say. 'It's being fixed up, done over, but as you'll soon find, nothing in India is done in a rush.'

Anxiously, Alexa twisted her engagement ring that was too heavy and too loose for her finger, despite being adjusted in London. 'You've had four months, James. I hope it's ready in time for our wedding.'

'Of course—and certainly when we return from honeymoon.'

'Talking of honeymoons,' Jonathan said artlessly, 'Harriet and I are about to retire so

67

we'll bid you good-night. Will we see you for tiffin, James?'

'Not until evening. I've a lot of work to clear before the week-end. George Bray is holding the fort in my absence and I want to leave him nothing more perplexing than whether to have beef or chicken curry for dinner.'

When their friends had gone, James put an arm about Alexa's slender waist and drew her close to him. 'At last! I thought we'd never be alone.'

'It wouldn't have been proper for Harriet to leave us last evening,' Alexa murmured. 'In fact, I'm surprised she did so now.'

'Ah! Jonathan's attraction plus a few extra nips at the little cologne bottle!'

'James!' Alexa looked up at him. The lamplight silvered his brown hair, and cast plains and shadows on his face so that she was reminded of the faded, sepia photograph of her papa standing stiff and proud in his ceremonial uniform.

'Oh, James, I do love you,' she whispered as she turned up her lips for his kiss. Their separation had unsettled her, but everything would be perfect now that they were together again.

His kiss was firm and when she tried to end it, he held her closer and his lips grew more possessive. It was the sort of kiss that Alexa had yearned for on the evening of their betrothal, but now she found it overwhelming.

'Darling Alexa,' he murmured huskily when he finally drew back. 'In just five days we'll be man and wife.'

At last, he was showing that he loved her, desired her, but when he took her chin and raised her face to his, she instinctively turned away her head. 'Please, James, it's—it's so dreadfully hot.'

He was holding her too tightly and although she tried to break away, he again captured her lips with his. She fought panic, forcing herself to be still, not to struggle. It was like being kissed by a stranger.

Silently, she endured, desperately hoping that a spark would ignite within her so that she could respond as he wanted her to—as she wanted to. But finally, she wrenched away with a little cry. 'Please, James!'

He released her immediately, and said with a little laugh, 'Dearest Alexa! So beautiful, so young! But I can wait until we are married.'

She stared up at him. Her voice was low and intense. 'You do love me, don't you, James? Truly love me, I mean? Not just because I am—pretty?'

'Of course I do, silly! With all my heart! Don't be afraid of me, darling girl. I shall make you very happy, you'll see!'

As she watched him walk away, Alexa scolded herself angrily. What was wrong with her? James was everything she wanted. All she had ever dreamed of. How could she treat him so coldly? Despairing, she went into her room.

Seeta was sitting before the open window sewing lace on one of Alexa's petticoats. She rose and bowed as her mistress came in, her liquid brown eyes stealing a glance at her troubled face.

'Is all well, Miss-sahiba?' she asked softly as she helped Alexa undress.

'Very well, Seeta!' Alexa responded. 'The wedding is set for Tuesday.'

As Alexa stepped gratefully out of the dress, Seeta, who seemed strangely agitated, suddenly cried, 'Forgive me, Miss-sahiba, but I must ask. Is it—is it true that the widows of soldiers killed in the Crimea are being brought here to marry our zamindars, our landowners?'

Alexa looked at her in astonishment. 'I shouldn't think so for one minute. What on earth made you ask such an extraordinary thing?'

Seeta averted her face. 'It is being whispered in the bazaars, Miss-sahiba. It is said that the Europeans are going to make us all Christians.'

Taken by surprise again, Alexa laughed. 'To be a Christian you must believe whole-heartedly in our God and in his word, Seeta. Our church has no need of unbelievers!'

The girl put her hands together, touched them first to her forehead and then to her chest, and bowed. But despite her meekness,

70

Alexa had a feeling that the ayah wasn't convinced.

'What else do they whisper in the bazaar?' she asked.

Seeta didn't answer until Alexa was seated at the dressing table. There was fear in her eyes as she whispered, 'They say there will be mutiny.'

The idea was startling. Alexa studied the girl in the mirror. 'What do you mean?' she asked, careful to keep her voice light.

'The East India Company is defiling the sepoys. They are greasing the new cartridges with cow and pig fat—the paper that the sepoys must bite before they can load their carbines. These are forbidden animals, Miss-sahiba.'

Alexa's eyebrows puckered as she watched the bent head in the mirror. How did Seeta know so much about sepoys? About guns?

'The Company is proud of its brave soldiers and wouldn't wish them harm.'

'They are trying to break their caste, Miss-sahiba!'

Alexa turned on the stool so that she could look directly at the frightened girl. 'Surely no-one really believes that? Why would the Company do such a thing?'

The dark head shook violently. 'It must be true, Miss-sahiba. Why else would they paint the cartridges with the vile fat?'

Alexa strived to recall pat words of her

father's. Often she had heard him say that to the Indian, caste was everything. It governed the whole society of India.

'Do the regimental officers know of these rumours?'

'The sepoys have told them. The officers say that the fat is mutton. That the soldiers need not bite the cartridge papers, but tear them open.'

'If the officers say that the fat is mutton, then it is so!'

'The sepoys say that the officers are duped by the arsenal at Dum Dum,' Seeta offered. 'They have deceived them as they are deceiving the sepoys. They will not handle the cartridges, Miss-sahiba. they will mutiny!'

Alexa turned back to the mirror, staring with unseeing eyes at her reflection as the brush again moved through her hair. This conversation in the hot, subtropical night was totally unreal. She couldn't believe that she was sitting here calmly discussing such terrible things as defilement, the breaking of caste, and mutiny. Ladies simply didn't talk of such things.

But the frightful prospect could not be lightly dismissed. If the unrest among the sepoys was such public knowledge that even an ayah knew of it, not only the officers but James—as an official of the Company—must know of it, too. He had said nothing to her, so he couldn't be worried. The misunderstanding about the grease used on the cartridges was serious, but was doubtlessly being settled as a matter of urgency.

CHAPTER SIX

The strange, unsettling talk with Seeta in the quiet of the night seemed even more unreal in the light of day. When questioned, James dismissed the rumours as unfounded bazaar gossip, and Alexa, who had refused to reveal her source, was reassured.

The evenings were given to James, but during the day, the ladies of the station vied to welcome her. Luncheons and tea parties were arranged by those anxious to glean the latest news from home.

'Please continue to use the carriage, Alexa,' Jonathan said the morning before her wedding. 'James must buy one for you when you return. Who is hostess today?'

'Mrs Angus McFee. She's a fabled hostess, Harriet says. Do you know, Jonathan, although there are lots of servants in my childhood memories, I never fail to be surprised by the sheer number each household employs? What with butlers, bearers, ayahs, cooks, grooms, sweepers ... The list is endless.'

'And all necessary, my dear. At first sight it seems decadent, but behind every house-servant is a dependent family. In Lucknow alone, their number runs into the thousands.' Jonathan bent and kissed her cheek. 'Now off you go!'

The McFee bungalow was surrounded by lawns surprisingly green for the time of year. The rooms were large with wide windows designed to catch the slightest movement of air.

Marbeth McFee, a willowy woman in her mid-thirties who managed to look cool and elegant despite the heat, welcomed Alexa warmly. There were six other ladies present, all of whom she had already met and Alexa was lauded and fussed over—and enjoyed the spoiling.

The talk eventually turned to the mock mediaeval tournament to be held that evening. Many of the ladies had designed costumes specially for the occasion, but Alexa confessed that she had only normal evening wear.

'I'd no idea you went in for such exotic entertainment. Polo and pig-sticking were the highlights in my parents' day.'

'An idea of Mrs Withers, the colonel's wife,' Marbeth McFee told her. 'She attended one on leave in Warwickshire, and brought the idea back with her. It immediately appealed to the younger officers, and—with a little pressure from us ladies who longed for something new—the general gave permission to try it. It was a howling success from the first. The men like the dressing up as much as we do, and they enjoyed the physical side even more! There have been a few broken bones, but nothing too serious, so it's now an institution.'

'I do wish James had told me for I could have devised a costume,' Alexa said, vexed.

'I'll give you a conical hat with ribbons,' Mrs McFee promised. 'Wear something diaphanous with wide sleeves and you will make a perfect Lady Guinevere.'

'I have a fine, plaited belt woven with beads that you can have,' Mrs Edwards said. She had been Alexa's hostess the previous day. 'I'll send one of my people over with it this afternoon. You will be the belle of the tournament!'

Alexa was overwhelmed. 'Thank you! You are all so kind!' Somewhat shyly, but eager to return their hospitality, she added, 'When James and I return from honeymoon, you must all come to luncheon at our bungalow.'

There was a tinkling little laugh. 'I do hope he's taken better control of his servants and cleaned the place up. I cannot imagine anyone actually eating luncheon in James's bungalow. There isn't a table that doesn't wobble and scarcely a chair that isn't covered in books and saddlery!'

All eyes riveted on the speaker, Vivienne Davis, a light-haired young woman with slanting, green eyes in a pert face. There was an electric silence in which the girl pouted, glanced slyly at Alexa, tossed a defiant head and looked away.

Then, everyone was talking at once, but as

76

Alexa strived to look attentive, she was aware that something had just occurred that she knew nothing of. She knew little about Vivienne Davis except that her husband commanded a Native Infantry Regiment. She wasn't beautiful, scarcely pretty, but there was something sensual in that pert face with its sleepy green eyes.

Alexa wondered suddenly if Vivienne and James had had an affair. Or was she just being mischievous? There were many bored, lonely wives, and some might find teasing a newcomer amusing. James was a handsome man, but surely too honourable to indulge in such an illicit relationship?

Annoyed that she should have harboured such a thought, Alexa fixed her mind on the conversation. But when the party was over, with memories of James declaring that his bungalow was being 'fixed up', she decided to go and see how the work was progressing.

She discovered a long building badly in need of a coat of paint, with an open veranda on three sides. It was fronted by an uninspired patch of garden that shimmered in the heat. An elderly gardener squatted among the rows as motionless as the wilting plants that surrounded him. He seemed to be the only person around.

The carriage stopped at the front steps and the driver assisted Alexa to alight. Clearly offended by the lack of welcome, he stalked off around the back of the house in search of the servants.

Alexa walked up the steps and through the open doorway. The room she entered was stiflingly hot and typical of many bachelor households, containing the usual hotchpotch of small furniture surrounding a cane sofa and long chairs.

Mrs Davis had been right about the papers and books which seemed to cover every surface, but not about the saddlery—in fact, the room was not as untidy as Alexa had feared, but there was no sign of the promised 'fixing up' or 'doing over'!

Sweeping a pile of magazines to the floor, she sat down on the sofa just as James's butler hurried in, salaaming and beaming all over his wrinkled face.

'Welcome, welcome, Miss-sahiba! I am Ali,' he cried, obviously knowing exactly who she was. 'Pardon me—I was busy with very important work. You will take tea?'

'Is there lemonade?'

'Immediately, Miss-sahiba!' The butler departed and moments later his raised voice could be heard yelling in Hindustani. There was a sharp yelp from somewhere at the rear of the bungalow and the ceiling fan jerked into action. A sweeper appeared like magic and began to whisk the veranda while the gardener hoed the flowerbeds with great industry.

Ali was back in a trice, a glass of lemonade

on a silver salver that badly needed polishing—
but it was surprisingly good lemonade!

While Alexa was drinking it, the butler
hovered, telling her of the wonderful
transformation the bungalow was about to
undergo ready for the new Memsahib
Brunswick. The whitewash, the rugs and the
furniture. 'Everything a memsahib's heart
could wish for! The sahib has promised.'

'I'm sure it will be very nice, Ali.' Alexa
smiled, amused. She had obviously caught the
servants very much on the hop.

'I must go now,' she said to Ali's obvious
relief.

As she rose to her feet, she felt a sharp prick
in her hand where it rested on a cotton rug
draped over the back of the sofa. She snatched
her hand away, and with a cry of triumph, Ali
wrestled free a small object that was enmeshed
in the loose weave.

'Memsahib Davis's ear-ring,' he cried
holding it aloft. 'We have searched for many
days. And now you have found it, Miss-sahiba.
The sahib will be most pleased. Memsahib
Davis will be most pleased—' He caught
Alexa's eye, broke off in confusion and
dropped his gaze.

In the silence, Alexa took the pearl and
diamond ear-ring from him, looked at it a
moment then dropped it on to the salver. She
said quietly, 'Tell the sahib that you found it
when you were cleaning, Ali.'

He bowed. 'Yes, Miss-sahiba!'

As she was driven back to the Residency, Alexa thought about the ear-ring. Nothing in itself, but together with Vivienne Davis's sly look and suggestive laughter, perhaps everything. The suspicion that Mrs Davis and James had been more than friends returned.

Alexa had already decided that James's past had no part in their future together but Ali's words, spoken so impulsively, could not be easily banished. 'We have searched for many days . . . ' Days, and she and James had been betrothed for months. But she didn't want to believe that James had betrayed her. The loss must have occurred during a social call.

Back at the Residency, Alexa met with Harriet who promised to accompany her to the church that evening.

'I have every intention of coming, Alexandra. Sadly, your mother cannot be here, but I am pleased to take her place. You've become like a daughter to me.'

'Thank you, Harriet!' Alexa impulsively hugged her very dear friend. 'That's one of the greatest compliments anyone has ever paid me!'

The last rays of the sun coloured the church roof as Alexa and Harriet walked across the courtyard towards the south porch. 'I hope the dear old boy gets a move on,' Harriet said. 'We must attend the tournament tonight. Everyone will be there and it will be great fun.'

Reverend Anderson was seated on the porch bench sorting through a pile of hymn books from which rose the musty smell of mildew.

'A sorry state,' the padre said, shaking his head. 'And everything will be worse when the rains come.' He abandoned the mouldering books and rose to his feet. 'So good of you to come, ladies.'

Alexa had gone to the arched doorway and was peering around the ill-lit church. 'Haven't Mr Brunswick and Mr Waldicott arrived?'

'No doubt they will!' Reverend Anderson cocked his head like a chubby bird. 'I do believe they are here!'

Mrs Waldicott and her daughters were also in the carriage that clattered across the yard. The group came into the porch with a rush, Mrs Waldicott propelling her off-spring before her.

I do so hope we're not late,' she exclaimed. 'Ayah mislaid my blue gloves and I had to change my entire outfit. She's been hopeless these last few weeks. Restless, jumpy as a kitten before a thunderstorm.'

She paused for breath, blinked apologetically and said. 'This is Faith, and this is Hope. Curtsy to Mrs Symonds and Miss Denton, girls.'

The two, alike as the proverbial peas and as pretty as china dolls, curtsied dutifully, their dark, shoe-button eyes fixed in bright expectancy upon Alexa.

Alexa studied them warily. They looked intelligent enough not to tread on her gown, drop her train or lose the bouquets, but those sparkling dark eyes in the angelic faces spelled mischief brewing. She leaned and whispered to them and the girls nodded vigorously.

The party went into the church, wrinkling their noses at its musty smell.

'What did you promise them?' Harriet whispered as they took their places.

'Bicycles, with bells and panniers,' Alexa whispered back, looking around the shadowy building where candles fought valiantly against the rapidly encroaching darkness. Alexa shivered. Tomorrow morning, in this place, for better or worse, Alexandra Denton would cease to exist and Alexandra Brunswick would take her place. Her life would be inextricably linked with James's for ever.

She looked up at his profile, calm and sure in the candle light, and sensing her gaze he turned and smiled down. It will be all right, she thought, it's got to be all right.

The rehearsal proceeded smoothly, but everyone sighed with relief when it was over and they were free to troop out into the night air. As they walked back across the courtyard, James squeezed Alexa's hand where it rested in the crook of his arm. 'This time tomorrow, we'll be on our way to Kashmir as man and wife,' he said softly.

'Come on, you two,' Harriet called. 'We don't want the tournament to start without us. I've reserved the best seats and it's time we claimed them.'

As the carriage bowled towards the polo grounds where the tournament was being held, James said quietly to Alexa, 'Thank you for finding Vivienne's earring.' He gave her arm a little squeeze. 'Neville—Captain Davis—was most upset at its loss. The pair were an anniversary gift. He was demented when we couldn't find it. Practically tears my bungalow apart every time they call. Poor Ali is terrified of him.'

Alexa was glad that the darkness hid her blush. The explanation was quite plausible, and she believed him—of course she believed him! 'Ali told you of my visit? I should have waited until the refurbishment. I hope you don't mind?'

'Just sorry you had to see it in such a state, but it will be a show-house by the time we return!' And he leaned under cover of the darkness and swiftly kissed her cheek.

A band was playing lustily when they entered the grounds, which were brilliantly lit by a hundred flares. Ranks of packed benches were ranged alongside the 'list' and the party claimed the centre seats which Harriet had coerced one of the organising officers into keeping for them.

Alexa, resplendent in a lavender gown, and

the pretty conical hat and the beaded belt, looked around with keen interest. Circular tents were erected at each end of the list, their long flags streaming in the evening breeze. Outside the tents were long lances, piled tripod fashion, in the charge of liveried pages.

The thrilling bellow of trumpets echoed across the field of chivalry as the first of the knights came from their respective tents. They were clad in authentic-looking armour, their heads concealed beneath lumped helmets.

The cheering grew in volume as the adversaries took up their stations at each end of the list. The trumpets blared again and at a signal from the regally attired Tournament King, who was, James confided in a whisper, 'Colonel Withers of the 49th,' the two lowered their lances and charged.

Five hundred voices roared encouragement as the two big horses thundered towards each other, divided only by a low rail. There was an almighty crash as lances struck shields and the two knights flew from their saddles to land ignobly in the dust. 'Boo, a draw!' the crowd yelled, unsportingly.

Two fresh knights came from the tents and were duly mounted and armed. Again they sought a favour from their ladies, and again the crowd roared as they thundered down on each other with lowered lances. This time, the green knight easily unseated his rival, the white, and there was great rejoicing among those who had wagered successfully on the outcome.

The antagonists in the third bout sported red and purple plumes. When they rode along the ranks of spectators, the red knight reined his horse before the Symonds' party and lowered his lance to Alexa. Startled, she looked up at the knight, looming huge in his armour, aware that the crowd was gasping at his audacity for they all knew that she was to marry James the next morning.

With an outraged oath, James rose to his feet, but Alexa saw only the eyes shining down at her from behind the knight's visor. Impulsively, she took the lavender ribbon from around her throat and quickly tied it to the lance.

'Alexa!' James exclaimed, but Alexa only saw the red knight as he saluted her and galloped back to the list.

'For goodness' sake, Alexa, how could you be so flirtatious?' her fiancé demanded. 'I'll have that man demoted for his impertinence, whoever he is.' But his voice was lost beneath the roar of the crowd.

Red knight charged purple. The clash as they met deafened the ears as it reverberated around the field. For a moment, it seemed that neither would fall. Then the purple knight reeled and fell, ungainly, from the saddle. The victorious red knight wheeled his charger, saluted the Tournament King, and galloped from the field into the thick darkness.

'Who was that man? Who was that?' James demanded of everyone in earshot, but no-one knew and when the next contestants appeared, no-one cared. Only Alexa, who couldn't forget the massive bulk of her knight and his shining eyes.

The festivities were a roaring success and still going strong when the Symonds' party returned to the Residency. Harriet wouldn't allow James to come in with them. 'Go and have a drink with your friends and let Alexa have an early night. But remember, James, sober and on time at the church!'

'I'll make sure of it,' Hugh promised. Alexa was relieved to see that he was taking his duties as groom's-man very seriously.

James bent and kissed Alexa chastely upon the cheek. 'Until tomorrow, then! Sleep well, my dear.'

When the women were alone, Harriet said, 'Are you sure of what you are doing, Alexandra? The knot, once tied, is a tight one and difficult if not impossible to undo.'

'Of course I'm sure, Harriet!'

Harriet's hazel eyes were sharp as they rested on Alexa's face. 'On the journey, you talked much of your longing for India. Of your desire for a marriage as close and happy as that of your parents. Of James's !ikeness to your adored papa. But you were not so forthcoming about James himself!'

Alexa flushed. 'Some things are personal and not to be discussed, even with a good friend.' She looked out of the window at the lights of the city. 'But I do love him, Harriet. I do, I do!'

Harriet said drily, 'It's me you're trying to convince, not yourself.'

Alexa was silent, remembering that Gideon had asked much the same questions in Hyde Park, and on the road from Calcutta.

Finally, she said, 'My parents expect us to be married tomorrow. I'm to telegraph them as soon as the ceremony is over.'

'I am aware of your parents' wishes,' Harriet responded, somewhat impatiently, 'but you've grown up, Alexandra. You're not the child who boarded the ship at Tilbury. You're a woman now, so listen to your heart, my dear. And know that Jonathan and I are always here for you.'

Despite the brandy that Harriet insisted upon, Alexa couldn't sleep. This was the last night she would spend as a single woman. She wondered if her parents were thinking of her? She longed for their presence. At no time in her young life had she missed them more.

It was a relief when morning came and Seeta arrived bearing a tray with fresh fruit and lemon tea. Alexa drank the tea gratefully but could eat nothing.

She bathed and then, powdered and scented and wrapped in a loose gown, sat before the

87

mirror while Seeta dressed her hair. When it was done, the ayah took a long hooked pole and carefully lifted down the bridal gown and spread it upon the bed. It was time for Alexa to dress.

Slowly, the ritual proceeded. The corsets, the hooped cage, the petticoats and finally the dress itself. Looking at herself in the mirror, Alexa gasped. She saw a stranger; a slender stranger, ethereal in the lovely white gown. A stranger with chestnut hair curled and looped about her face.

'Miss-sahiba, you look so beautiful,' Seeta cried, her dark eyes glowing with delight. 'But so pale. Let me touch some colour in your cheeks and lips.'

'Thank you, Seeta.'

The ayah was arranging the veil when there was an urgent pounding on the door. 'Who is it?' Alexa cried, agitated by the rude interruption to her preparations.

'It's me! James! Open the door!'

'James? What are you doing here? You can't come in! You mustn't see me before the ceremony! It's unlucky! Go away!'

'I must see you! It's very important. Alexa, open the door!'

'Go away, James!'

But he persisted and, in the end, Alexa told Seeta to open the door a crack while she stood concealed behind it. James, however, pushed the door wide and came into the room. He was

88

flushed with excitement. He stopped short when he saw Alexa, and stared, awe-struck. Then he collected himself and blurted, 'My dear, forgive me. I have the most distressing news. I've been ordered to leave immediately for Meerut.'

'I don't understand!' Alexa cried. 'We are to be married in an hour.'

'I know—and I'm broken-hearted. That my orders should come now, on our wedding day, is cruel. But I must go immediately. I have no choice. Horses are waiting downstairs—I should have been on the road hours ago.'

He made as though to take her in his arms, but she moved quickly back. 'Forgive me, Alexa! We'll be married the minute I'm free, I promise.' When she didn't speak, he said again, 'Believe me, I'm devastated, but I must go!'

He turned and she heard his running footsteps in the corridor, receding rapidly into distance. Alexa closed the door then, and leaned weakly against it.

'Oh, Miss-sahiba,' Seeta whispered, horrified by the turn of events. She was appalled to see the scalding tears that streamed down her young mistress's cheeks, and burying her face in a corner of her sari, wept in sympathy.

The gentle, young ayah was not to know that the tears shed by Alexa were tears of sheer relief.

CHAPTER SEVEN

'You can't stay in Luknow on your own,' Harriet declared. 'Jonathan must get back to the hospital and there's a thousand things awaiting my attention in Delhi, so you will come with us!'

She speared a piece of kidney and regarded it with suspicion. 'Jonathan says that James is attending a court-marshal at Meerut. The Company regards it as extremely serious—hence James's untimely dispatch—so it's likely to drag out for weeks. So go pack your trunks. I won't hear any argument!'

Alexa looked gratefully across the breakfast table at her companion. 'I'd like to come—if you're sure I won't be in the way?'

'Then it's settled! We leave in the morning.'

When they rose from the table, Harriet said, 'While we are in Lucknow, we might as well visit some of the sights. But first, please excuse me for an hour. I've a letter to write. Wait for me on the veranda, will you?'

Alexa was embarrassed to go alone to face those who regularly frequented the courtyard for many were to have been guests at her wedding. The thought of accepting their sympathy, of acting a disappointment she didn't feel, filled her with guile. Strangely enough, Harriet had offered neither, but had accepted the news with an impatient click of her tongue.

'You can't hide for ever, Alexandra. Go out and face the world,' Harriet commanded when she confessed her reluctance.

So Alexa went, trying to look as crestfallen as any girl whose marriage had been rudely cancelled without warning. She forgot the rôle however when she saw the man leaning on the rail, looking out across the courtyard. Tall and broad, his dark, unruly hair almost crackling with vitality, there could be no mistaking Gideon Masters.

Unprepared for the encounter, her step faltered. For a moment, she wondered if Harriet had arranged this. Then she collected herself and walked to the far end of the veranda.

Almost immediately, Gideon's cheerful voice spoke behind her. 'Good-morning, Miss Denton! And I have no intention of expressing any regret that you are still Miss Denton. It's the best news I've had all year.'

She spun on him, her dark eyes flashing. 'Then your year has been very dull, lieutenant!' Aware of heads turning, she modulated her voice. 'I thought you had left Lucknow. You don't seem in a hurry to rejoin your regiment.'

'I've been entrusted with several missions along the way which I am doing my best to fulfil.' His smoky eyes kindled with a teasing light. 'Why, I do believe you suspect me of absconding, Alexa, of deserting my post.'

Her cheeks grew rosy beneath those laughing eyes. 'Nothing of the sort! But there are few soldiers, I wager, who would not relish such leisurely missions!'

'Please don't suggest that to the Paymaster General. I fear he'll dock my pay for tardiness, if not for dereliction of duty.' He was openly laughing at her now, and she furled her parasol, fighting a tremendous urge to hit him with it.

'But don't let's quarrel,' he said quickly, keeping a wary eye on the parasol. 'I'm pleased to find you here for it saves me having to seek you out.'

Alexa glanced at him suspiciously. They hadn't spoken or met face-to-face since that night beside the Ganges, but that one, swift glance was enough to tell her that his smile still had the same disturbing effect on her.

'Why should you wish to see me, Mr Masters?' she asked loftily.

He didn't answer at once and in the silence she was so intensely aware of him that she fancied she could feel his breath upon her cheek although he stood several feet away.

He sighed. 'We parted with some bitterness, didn't we, Alexa? But can't we forget the hostility between us? Declare a truce?'

'I didn't know we were hostile to each other,' she said in a low voice. 'We disagreed, but I hope we are not enemies.'

'I am forever your friend!' he said gently. 'I'd like to be more, but you've made it plain that it's not to be. So it's as a friend I speak now.' His voice strengthened, became urgent. 'Please leave Lucknow, Alexa, leave the plains, go to the hills for a while. Bad things are happening at Meerut and throughout Bengal. Like the kindling in a tinder-box, they can start a fire that will only be extinguished at a terrible cost.'

She looked into his eye where all laughter had gone and didn't pretend to misunderstand. 'You think there'll be a mutiny, Gideon? My ayah warned me. But I've discussed this with James and Hugh Waldicott and they are convinced that such a thing is impossible.'

Taking her arm, he led her to where chairs were set around a table, motioning to a vendor to bring tea. Only when the cups were before them did he speak.

'I'm sure they're sincere in their beliefs. Many officers of native regiments regard the sepoys as their children.' His voice grew grim. 'But they are not children, and no matter how much they respect their officers—and not all do for there are as many bad as there are good—the sepoys sense a threat to their caste, to their whole society. Their allegiance to these is stronger than any loyalty they feel towards British officers and a foreign Company.'

Alexa's voice was almost pleading. 'But it's all being put right. Compromises are already in place. James said so.'

Exasperated, Gideon ran a hand through his hair. 'I wish you had as much faith in me,' he said almost angrily. 'Few are taking this threat seriously. Terrible blunders are being made. Go to the hills, Alexa, where you'll be safe.'

Alexa's chin came up at his commanding tone. She wouldn't be bullied! If matters were so serious, Harriet would know of it. Or the Surgeon Major. Gideon was being too cautious! She stole a glance at him. Strong and sure and steady, she knew in her heart that he wasn't a man to take fright at shadows. There was fear in his eyes, but the fear was for her, not for himself.

'I'm leaving Lucknow tomorrow,' she said too quickly, too loudly. 'I'm going to Delhi with the Symonds, and then to Kashmir on honeymoon!'

Gideon rose to his feet. His face was expressionless. 'If that's what it takes to remove you from danger, then so be it! I wish you every happiness.'

He was leaving! She said quickly, 'Harriet and I are sightseeing in the city. Will you escort us, Gideon?'

'Time presses, I'm afraid. Goodbye, Alexa! It may be that I shall see you in Delhi.' But it was said politely and with no enthusiasm.

'Gideon!' she called after him. 'Tell me, are

you my red knight?'

But he was striding away and, watching him go, she had the overwhelming desire to weep . . .

The outing to the great houses and palaces of Lucknow failed to inspire her. More than once she found herself wishing that the lieutenant was with them and scolded herself for such foolishness. The postponement of her marriage to James was a relief, and she wouldn't pretend otherwise, but there was no real estrangement. Falling in love with a stranger—even as attractive a stranger as Lieutenant Gideon Masters—was not part of her plans, but she was honest enough to admit that she was in very real danger of doing just that.

His attraction would surely fade in time. After all, James was handsome, too!

They were ready to travel at five the following morning. The women had expected bullock carts, but Jonathan indicated a different mode of transport.

'Elephants!' Alexa's eyes shone as she stared at the great beasts with their jewelled harness and silk-fringed howdahs.

'I thought you would appreciate the loftier view, and air clear of milling dust,' Jonathan told them as they climbed into the howdahs. 'You'll also find the motion most relaxing once you're used to it.'

The first elephant moved out of the

95

courtyard with a stride that covered the ground at a—surprising speed, and the second animal, carrying the servants, followed behind. A luggage cart brought up the rear of the little procession.

They passed through the busy city and out once more on to the highway that led to Cawnpore, and to the Grand Trunk Rood.

There was a strong feeling of déjà vu as they travelled. There was the well-remembered variety of transport, the motley crowd of travellers, the early starts, the long encampments in the oppressive heat of midday when the dusty road fell suddenly silent and deserted. And in the soft darkness, the string of camp fires that stretched in an unbroken chain from Calcutta to Peshawar.

But there was no officer on a big white horse, no talks beside the camp fire. Alexa was grateful for she needed a settled mind and the chance to turn again to thoughts of James, to recapture her love for him.

Dear James, she thought sleepily as the sway of the howdah lulled her senses. She pictured him standing beside the fireplace in the library at Whitmore Square, tall, straight, distinguished. But it was of Gideon that she dreamed . . .

The Symonds' house was a two-storeyed building on Amritsar Road. Alexa was given a room with a view over gardens and a small ornamental lake. As Seeta was unpacking, a

96

servant brought a packet to Alexa.

'This came an hour ago, Miss-sahiba.'

It was a letter from James. Jonathan had telegraphed Meerut to tell him of their plans, and he declared himself delighted that she was moving with the Symonds to Delhi.

It is so much closer to Meerut, he had written. *A mere forty miles, and as soon as this disgraceful business here is over, I shall be with you in a matter of hours. We'll be married in Delhi and proceed on our honeymoon as planned. It was a great disappointment, the postponement of our wedding, but don't be despondent, dearest. A few more days, and I'll be with you! Our lives together will really begin.*

Alexa put the letter in her writing case. Everything will be all right, she told herself firmly. Looking out over the lake where the setting sun set a path of flame across the placid water, she inexplicably shivered.

The deep notes of a dinner gong sounded, bringing Alexa from her reverie, and she went downstairs.

The invitations to the Grand Ball at the royal palace the next Saturday had arrived in the Symonds' absence. It was addressed to the Surgeon Major and Mrs Symonds and guests and, over dinner, Harriet urged Alexa to join them.

'It's short notice, I know, but these things are often so much more enjoyable when there's no time to fuss over one's appearance.' Harriet said. 'I shall wear the purple gown I bought in London, and you have that beautiful ivory silk you wore aboard ship, Alexandra. We have jewels, gloves and slippers so there's no need to spend hours shopping. It will be the most relaxing ball I've ever attended.'

'I'd love to come! I adore to dance and have never attended a function in a royal palace before—only a garden party. I was presented to Her Majesty.'

'You'll like King Bahadur Shah! He's eighty-two years old now and has little real power, poor dear, but he's a most tolerant and hospitable monarch, much loved and respected by everyone. His Grand Balls really are grand, though the band isn't always in key—but nobody minds.'

'It sounds fun,' Alexa said. 'Will it be well attended?'

'Alexandra, simply everyone will be there.'

Jonathan hired a landau for the occasion. At eight o'clock on Saturday evening they drove through the wide streets of Delhi to the vastness of the palace. It was lit with a thousand lights so that it could be seen far out on the southern plain, and in the hills to the north of the city known as the Ridge.

The great, public apartments were already crowded, the brilliant silks and satins of the ladies and the native dignitaries interwoven by the scarlets, blues and greens of uniforms, and by the sober broadloom of the civilian gentlemen.

Jewels flashed in the turbans of princes, cascaded from the ears and throats of ladies. It was a dazzling scene of opulence and wealth.

'It's all display,' Harriet whispered to Alexa from behind her fan. 'Many of the princes live very simply and others depend entirely upon the King's generosity.'

They had moved forward in the receiving line and now faced their host, Bahadur Shah II, King of Delhi. He welcomed the Symonds warmly before turning to Alexa. She curtsied deeply and when she rose, found herself looking into a pair of piercing, dark eyes set in a thin, ageing face where wisdom and kindness were etched.

'Welcome to the palace, Miss Denton.' The King's English was excellent. 'We are delighted to have you with us.'

'Thank you, Your Majesty,' Alexa replied softly.

'A new face—and a very pretty face—is always welcome. My good friends the Surgeon Major and his dear wife must bring you to dine one evening, and then we can talk a little. Please enjoy the ball tonight.'

'Thank you, Your Majesty!'

She curtsied and moved on to where Harriet and Jonathan waited. The three went into an immense chamber where a sextet of musicians played a Viennese waltz and many couples danced beneath the glitter of crystal chandeliers.

Harriet and Jonathan seemed to know everyone. Alexa was introduced to a bewildering variety of partners and soon found herself dancing with a spritely merchant. Then she danced with a very young Cornet of Horse, newly arrived from Bombay to join the garrison at Kurnaul. There followed a distinguished, much-bewhiskered gentleman who was an equerry to the King.

The Symonds reclaimed her and they went on to supper which was as lavish and exotic as the ball itself. She was toying with the seventh course when she looked across the room and into the eyes of Gideon Masters.

The fork slipped unnoticed from her fingers as they looked at each other for what seemed an age. Then Jonathan touched her arm and drew her attention to the crocodile of graceful young girls in saris who each bore a gilded tray of fruit upon her head. When she looked back, Gideon was gone. Her eyes searched for him in vain and she was shocked at the intensity of her disappointment.

After supper, she danced with a handsome and entertaining young prince who had, he told her, learned to dance at Oxford University.

And then, without warning, she was whisked away by a man taller than most, broader than most, the planes of whose face seemed carved from oak. The musicians were again playing a waltz and they whirred across the floor.

Alexa looked up at her partner, looked into those smoky-grey eyes and couldn't look away. They danced until it was time to clear the floor.

Gideon took Alexa's hand and led her out on to the terrace where moonlight filtered through lattice and fountains sprayed perfumed water into pools where lotus flowers blossomed.

'It's so unreal—like a wonderful dream. I've never known anywhere as beautiful,' Alexa said as they looked out over the moon-washed city.

'Beautiful, yes, and cruel. The heat, the flies, the droughts, the floods after the monsoons, the poverty. They are also India!'

She smiled up at him. 'Don't pretend! You love this country, as I do. There's nowhere on earth I'd rather be.'

He touched her hair, letting a gleaming strand curl about his fingers. 'There's no-one on earth I'd rather be with,' he said softly. 'I want to share my life with you, Alexa, but you're not free. And even if you were, I couldn't be so selfish. I truly wish you out of it.'

She turned up her face, gazing into his eyes. 'Do you, Gideon?' she asked.

He touched her cheek. 'You must know that your happiness is my happiness, Alexa. Your life is my life. Follow your heart, my darling!'

His face was only inches away from hers and the exciting prickle of danger raced her nerve endings. She felt as if she were drowning. 'Oh, Gideon!'

When he touched her lips with his she had neither the strength nor the desire to resist. Her lips answered him as eagerly as they had beside the moonlit Ganges. When at last he put her from him and walked with her to the archway that led to the ballroom, she had ceased to think of the proprieties. She knew now, that being with Gideon was the most right and natural thing in the world.

He stopped in the doorway. 'I'm sorry, Alexa! I had no right . . . No-one should look as beautiful as you do tonight. It isn't fair. Please forgive me! Harriet and Jonathan are over there by the alcove. Go and join them, please.'

'But aren't you . . . ?'

He shook his head. 'I must go and I'd rather slip away quietly.'

Dismayed, she looked up at him. 'When will I see you again? Harriet has a bridge party tomorrow after tiffin. Will you come? You needn't play—'

'I won't be here. I must be in Meerut by morning.'

'Then you'll see James,' she cried without thinking, then blushed with embarrassment for she had just betrayed her fiancé in the most blatant manner.

Gideon didn't seem to notice. 'I doubt it! Stay close to Harriet and Jonathan, Alexa. Stay close to the house.' He bowed courteously and was gone.

Numbed by his sudden departure and by the kisses he had no right to bestow or she to receive, Alexa rejoined her friends. She avoided Harriet's questioning eyes and gave thanks that the Surgeon Major was particularly unobservant when he was discussing Asian antiquities, as he was now with the Rajah of Hyderabad.

The Symonds made their departure soon after. If either noticed that their young guest was exceptionally quiet, neither commented. Nor did they ask questions next day when she declined to join the bridge party, pleading a headache, and found a shady spot in the garden to read.

It was in the early evening, when they were enjoying the evening breeze, that the butler, Jawan, announced a visitor from Meerut.

Alexa jumped to her feet with a glad cry and Gideon's name on her lips—thankfully unuttered for it was James who came striding in. He looked flustered as he shook Jonathan's hand, kissed Harriet's cheek and embraced Alexa.

'We didn't expect you so soon,' Jonathan said.

'The court-martial is over and the

punishment was carried out this morning so there seemed no point in staying,' James said. He flung himself into a chair and sprawled as though exhausted.

The others regarded him silently, the Symonds puzzled, Alexa in dismay, for to look at him now was to look at a stranger. The thought of spending her life with James filled her with panic.

At last, she looked into her heart and knew that she had never truly loved James. She had thought so at the time, back there in London, but it was all mixed up with his likeness to her father and her great desire to return to India. She had wronged him and must seize the first opportunity to beg his pardon and break their engagement. To return his ring . . .

Jonathan was asking about the court-martial.

'All eighty-five guilty. There could be no other verdict. They all disobeyed a direct order from their commanding officers to take the new cartridges. It was the sentences that were so unusual. We expected them to be disarmed, dismissed from their regiment and sent home.'

'Which is what usually happens,' Jonathan agreed.

'Not this time! They were sentenced to ten years' imprisonment with hard labour. This morning, they were paraded before the whole garrison, publicly stripped of their insignia, shackled by the ankles and marched off to the jail. Many were defiant, but others wept with shame. Some were old soldiers nearing pensionable age weighed down with medals. It was a sorry sight, and there was much angry murmuring in the ranks of sepoys. Trouble will come of this.'

'Will the sepoys mutiny?' Jonathan was asking.

'Mutiny is too drastic a word. The officers remain convinced of their men's loyalty. But the General will need to take swift and firm action just the same.' James shook his head in exasperation.

Alexa turned away. The word mutiny had struck fear into her heart. Gideon was in Meerut and whatever happened there, she sensed he would be in the thick of it. And she knew, without doubt, that she loved him. Loved him as she had never loved James . . .

CHAPTER EIGHT

Next morning, as Harriet and Alexa prepared for a shopping trip, Jawan came to tell them that there was a disturbance in the city. Jonathan had already left for the hospital in Delhi Garrison which lay beyond the Ridge, and James had gone down to the offices of the East India Company.

The women went out to the front veranda. 'Sounds like gunfire,' Harriet said, frowning. 'From the direction of the Rajghat Gate.'

'Could it be fireworks? Some sort of festival?'

Harriet shook her head. 'The servants would have asked for the day off. And, the King has forbidden the discharge of guns in the city. It's rioting, I'm afraid.'

Neither woman was particularly alarmed, for the gunshots were some distance away and lazy on the air like the popping of champagne corks.

'James thinks there will be trouble at Meerut following the imprisonment of the sepoys. Perhaps wind of it has reached Delhi.'

'Possibly. There are ruffians aplenty in the bazaars. No doubt they'd welcome an excuse to create mayhem. We'd better stay home today, give things time to settle.'

Harriet went indoors, but Alexa lingered.

She could hear shouting now. From several sections of the city, columns of smoke began to spiral into the morning sky. The disturbance was spreading, and rapidly.

She went back into the house and joined Harriet in the drawing-room.

'Whatever the trouble is, it's escalating.'

'I suspected it might,' Harriet said calmly. 'And because I'm a leery old woman who never takes unnecessary chances, I want you to go and pack a small bag—just valuables, documents, anything easy to carry, nothing that weighs. Oh, and change into something serviceable—and pack a shawl.'

Alexa didn't argue. Harriet was a shrewd woman who understood India better than most Europeans. She nodded and went up to her room.

Seeta was nowhere to be seen and didn't come when she was called, which was very unusual. With a puzzled frown, Alexa took a leather satchel from the cupboard and packed her jewellery and money, photographs and letters. She slipped James's ring back on to its gold chain and hung it about her neck. It was a family heirloom and she was responsible for its safety until it was returned.

With a cashmere shawl tucked into the top of the bag, and clad in a plain, grey dress, she went down through the house—a house unnaturally quiet.

She was crossing the hall when a horse came

galloping furiously up the driveway and skidded to a stop in a flurry of gravel. A rider almost fell from the saddle and came stumbling up the steps, calling as he came, 'Doctor Symonds, Doctor Symonds.'

'The doctor isn't here, Tom,' Harriet cried as she hurried across the hall. 'Can I be of help?'

The man clung to the doorpost without answering. He was grey beneath his tan and there was an angry bruise on his temple. His left arm was awkwardly held and the sleeve was torn and blood-soaked.

Harriet didn't waste any more time on questions.

'Help me get him to the study, Alexandra. I'd better take a look at him.'

Between them, the women got the slight figure of the injured man on to the sofa in Jonathan's study.

'It seems hardly the time,' Harriet said, 'but let me introduce a family friend. Mr Thomas Gillon, chief reporter on the *Delhi Gazette*. Tom, this is my good friend and charge, Miss Alexandra Denton.'

As she was making the introductions, Harriet helped Mr Gillon off with his coat, exposing the gaping cut on his forearm. She examined it with a professional eye.

'Jawan?' she called. 'Where is that lazy butler? Go to the kitchens, Alexandra, and rouse the servants. We need scissors, hot water, needle and thread, bandages.'

She was back in five minutes. 'The servants are all gone,' she said calmly. 'I couldn't find bandages, but I've brought a clean sheet.'

'Good girl!' Harriet was pleased to see that there was no panic in Alexa's manner as she tore the sheet into suitable strips and then, on impulse, thrust the remainder into her satchel.

'What happened, Tom?' Harriet asked as she washed the wound.

'Murder, Harriet. The native troops in Meerut have mutinied and are now in Delhi. They've been joined by every badmash and hooligan in the city.'

'They're rioting?'

'Worse! They're killing every European they come across, man woman and child. They attacked the *Gazette* offices and almost got me with a knife as I escaped through a rear window. The mob has gone crazy, torching buildings, looting, rampaging at will.'

'Where is the British regiment from Meerut?'

'Nowhere to be seen. There were only a handful to oppose the mutineers at the Rajghat Gate. Caught unprepared, they were soon cut down. We must flee the city at once.'

Harriet pushed aside the bowl of blood-stained water and turned to Alexa. 'Fetch me a bottle of Jonathan's whisky. He keeps it in the rosewood cabinet.'

The cabinet was locked so Alexa went back

109

to the kitchens and reappeared with an iron poker. Another minute and she had forced open the door and handed the bottle to Harriet.

To her surprise, Harriet didn't give a measure to the injured man, but poured the neat spirit liberally in and around the wound,

'Ahh, it stings like fury,' the reporter cried, arching against the cushions.

Harriet said calmly, 'A little trick of Jonathan's. He swears it helps the wound heal without becoming infected, so do keep still, Tom.' But she was not as heartless as she seemed for she poured a stiff measure into a glass and handed it to him before proceeding to thread the needle and stitch together the gaping edges of the wound.

Squeamishly averting her eyes, Alexa corked the remaining spirit and wedged the bottle down the side of her satchel. Then she left the room.

The stables were deserted of all but the horses. Undeterred, Alexa harnessed a pair of matched bays to the carriage. She filled two water bottles at the pump and then drove around the house to the front steps.

The noise of the rioting was very loud now. Somewhere close by, a house burned with a fierce crackling of timbers.

Alexa hurried indoors to help Harriet with Mr Gillon. The little reporter was apologetic as he leaned on their shoulders. Although still pale—as much from his ordeal with the needle as from loss of blood, Alexa suspected—he looked somewhat better than when he had arrived.

'Ladies, we must leave with all haste,' he urged, but Harriet insisted on a few minutes to fetch cushions to protect him as much as possible from the jolting over the rough roads.

It had been Alexa's intention to tie Mr Gillon's horse behind the carriage but it had either bolted or been stolen. With no time to look for it, she climbed to the box, took up the reins and sent the horses at a fast trot down the drive and on to the road, heading north towards the Ridge and the Delhi Garrison.

They turned into the Street of the Five Temples, and reined to an abrupt halt. Before them, from wall to wall, advanced a yelling multitude brandishing knives, staves and flaring torches. In the forefront, armed with carbines, were four sepoys. At sight of the three Europeans in the carriage, the sepoys shouted to their followers and the whole mob broke into a run, charging towards them.

Alexa wrenched the horses' heads around and they pranced and reared almost upsetting the carriage, but she got them around and with a crack of the whip sent them in full gallop back the way they had come.

Racing at full stretch, the matched pair soon left the pursuers behind and Alexa eased the horses to a trot.

They were in the western sector of the city and the streets were almost deserted. The few persons abroad scuttled swiftly along walls to vanish through doors that closed and locked behind them. Shutters were closed tight and an eerie silence lay over the normally busy streets.

Although they heard shouts and gunfire nearby, it wasn't until they were on the outskirts of the city that they encountered more rioters. A band was looting the shop of a Eurasian tailor and didn't notice the vehicle until it had come within twenty yards. Then a shout went up. Leaving the bolts of cloth strewn in confusion across the narrow alleyway, the band came whooping towards the carriage wielding staves and knives.

Alexa gritted her teeth. There could be no turning back in such narrow confines! Taking up the whip, she snapped it repeatedly about the horses' ears and they sprang into full gallop, the elegant little carriage rocking and swaying over the uneven ground so that Harriet and the reporter were forced to cling on tightly to prevent themselves being thrown head-long from the vehicle.

At the sight of the horses charging wildly down upon them, the rioters checked. Before they could re-group, the equipage drew level. Two vanished beneath the hooves, the others leaped back, flattening themselves against the walls. They slashed at the horses and the carriage as it passed, but Alexa's whip cracked among them, keeping them away just long enough for their blows to be ineffective. Then the vehicle was through and racing for open country.

Alexa kept the horses to a gallop until the city was no more than a long, white huddle behind them. She drew the team to a halt and waited until her heart had slowed its wild beat before she turned to her passengers.

'I hope Mr Gillon has survived the buffeting.'

'Perfectly, thank you, Miss Denton—and please call me Tom! Etiquette seems unimportant now. If those ruffians had taken hold of us . . . ' He shook his head in despair. 'The whole world has gone mad. Those who yesterday were our friends are now howling for our blood!'

He was in some pain and as though spent by the words, he closed his eyes and leaned back against the cushions.

Harriet glanced at him sharply, then retrieved one of the water bottles from beneath the seat. After lacing three tin cups with a small amount of the amber liquid from her cologne bottle, she poured a drink for each of them.

As Alexa sipped the tepid liquid, she looked about them. To the north, shimmering in the heat, was the dark silhouette of the Ridge. It crossed her mind to turn the carriage and drive overland towards the garrison which lay beyond it. Several thin columns of smoke, climbing skyward like graphite pencil marks, deterred her however, and she sought another avenue of escape.

'Which way?' she asked her companions.

Tom Gillon didn't open his eyes and Harriet didn't hear. She was lost in reverie and Alexa was forced to repeat the question.

Harriet started. 'Sorry, Alexandra! I was thinking of Jonathan.'

'Try not to worry, Harriet. At least he's safe at the hospital—but James went down into the city. He'll be in terrible danger. I've feared for them both since we first heard the rioting, but particularly for James.'

'James is resourceful. He'll save his skin,' Harriet declared confidently. 'But Jonathan— Jonathan will try to reach us. He'll go back to the house.'

'Not without taking half the garrison with him,' Alexa said stoutly.

With a frightened catch of breath, Alexa thought of Gideon Masters. Would Harriet be as reassuring about his safety as she was about James's, she wondered. She sighed and looked back at the road.

A little way ahead was a track running southward towards a dark smudge on the landscape which was probably a village. Tugging down her hat brim to shade her eyes against the glare, she studied the distant hamlet as a possible source of refuge.

Tom Gillon stirred and opened his eyes. 'Continue west, Miss Denton. Make for Kurnaul and the British lines. Where once we found help and kindliness without thought, we must now go warily, for goodness knows how far this uprising has spread. Or how many other stations have joined the mutiny. Until we discover otherwise, we must regard every village as hostile!'

Alexa took up the reins and they moved on into the setting sun, surprised to find how late it was, how fast the perilous hours had flown.

At dusk, they came to a hamlet—a meagre collection of huts surrounding a communal cooking fire. Stopping just outside the circle of light, the fugitives surveyed the area. It seemed deserted despite the fire and a steaming cooking pot which wafted a most alluring smell.

'Where is everyone?' Alexa whispered.

'Hiding I should think,' Harriet murmured.

Alexa clutched the whip, noticing that Tom Gillon had taken a revolver from his coat pocket.

Catching her glance, he smiled sheepishly. 'It's not loaded, I'm afraid, but it might discourage anyone who's watching.'

'That pot smells good,' Alexa said wistfully.

'We're all hungry,' the reporter admitted. 'But it would be wise to give this place a wide berth and camp the night on the plain.'

Before Alexa could turn the horses,

however, Harriet said sharply, 'Don't move!' And suddenly, they were surrounded!

Coming silent as ghosts from the darkness, perhaps a hundred in all, men, women and children, the villagers now formed a solid circle about the carriage.

Two men took hold of the horses' heads, and another motioned to the fugitives with the sickle he carried. 'Get down,' he said in Hindustani.

To argue was futile and dangerous. The three obeyed, but not without misgivings. They were instantly seized. The revolver was taken from Tom and the whip from Alexa and all three were subjected to a thorough search.

The carriage was driven away into the night and the prisoners taken before a zemindar, an old man who owned all the land around the village. He questioned them closely as to how one of them came to be hurt, and how they came to be driving at night across the great plain in a carriage slashed and scored.

They answered him honestly and the zemindar considered for a long time while they waited in great anxiety. Finally, he turned to the men who stood patiently in the doorway of his house. 'Give them food,' he said. 'And a hut in which to spend the night. And let nothing of this be told to any stranger.'

Then the old man turned to the fugitives. 'As a young man, I was a havildar with the 7th Regiment of Foot. Many are the battles I fought, and the honours I won. I still receive a pension from Queen Carriage. I have no quarrel with you. Tonight, you will be our guests, but you must leave at daybreak for fear that the mutineers will get wind of your presence and put the village to the torch.'

'Thank you, Sahib Zemindar. We are in your debt and shall not forget,' Harriet said, and Alexa and Tom Gillon agreed.

They were given food and mugs of piping hot tea. Then they were taken to a hut and given charpoys, beds made from a mesh of rope stretched on a wooden frame. In the morning, while it was still dark, after breakfasting on rice and chapattis, the carriage was brought from wherever the villagers had concealed it. The water bottles were filled at the well, the remaining rice and bread packed in a basket and placed in the carriage. The zemindar personally handed Tom the revolver which had now been loaded.

'Avoid the river road,' the old man cautioned. 'When you come to the fork, take the left hand for there are bands of dacoits, armed robbers, preying on travellers and no law to hinder them.'

The three gave heartfelt thanks to their hosts for their kindness. Harriet took her portmanteaux from the compartment behind the seat and presented the landowner with a generous gift of rupees. She then gave annas to all the children. Alexa's money was left intact for there were many miles yet to go and they might well have need of it. The reporter had only a few rupees in his pocket having lost his wallet in the skirmish at the *Gazette*.

Tom Gillon was much recovered after a sound sleep, but Alexa insisted upon driving the horses. They moved out on to the plain as the sun rose in the sky.

After an hour, they came upon an elderly couple stumbling across the plain carrying a blanket, but with neither food nor water. They greeted the carriage with cries of joy. They were, they said, Anthony and Jane Madoc and were fleeing from Faridabad.

'We had no time to pack. Fortunately, our carriage was waiting to take us into town, but we broke an axle during our flight, and then our horse was stolen,' Mrs Madoc said.

The couple were footsore and on the point of exhaustion and after drinking from the precious supply of water, they were levered into the carriage with Harriet, and Tom Gillon climbed to the driving seat beside Alexa.

They proceeded without incident and, an hour before noon, came to a fork in the road. Following the zemindar's instructions, they turned left away from the river and were soon among undulating country covered with low-growing scrub.

They stopped in the shade of a mango grove and tethered the horses where there was a little grazing. After sharing out the rice and two of the chapattis, they rested, dozing in the blazing heat of the afternoon. It was very quiet with only the buzzing of insects, the soft stamp of hooves, and Mr Madoc's gentle snores.

Alexa dreamed of England. Of a rented cottage on the banks of the Thames. Boating, the water cool against the hull, the distant lowing of cows, the snap of twigs . . . She came awake with a start. It was there again, the snap of a twig.

Tom Gillon was awake, crouched on one knee, revolver in hand. Without taking his eyes off the undergrowth, he motioned to Alexa and she quickly woke her sleeping companions, signalling for silence.

Tensely, they waited, but there was no further noise from the brush. They had begun to relax when, with blood-curdling yells, three men leaped suddenly from cover and fell upon the fugitives with staves and knives. Tom's revolver exploded once, twice, the reports deafening at such close quarters. It was a mad confusion of noise and bodies and cordite. Another shot, a scream—and it was over as quickly as it had begun.

Two of the attackers went crashing away through the brush. The third lay dead where he had fallen almost at Tom Gillon's feet.

There was a brief, shocked silence in which the sound of flight rapidly receded. As Tom bent to examine the fallen dacoit, Anthony Madoc murmured, 'We owe our lives to your

119

vigilance and courage, Mr Gillon.'

Alexa was about to speak when she caught sight of Harriet. The words died on her lips. Her friend was lying on the ground, a red flower blossoming on the front of her bodice. It took a moment to comprehend—then, with a cry of horror, Alexa flung herself down beside Harriet.

But Harriet Symonds was made of sterner stuff. She grasped Alexa's arm.

'Take hold, Alexandra! The blade has gone right through and seems to have missed the lung. But the bleeding must be stopped!'

Alexa fought rising hysteria. 'How? Tell me how?'

'The wounds must be plugged . . . pressure bandages applied. Tear one of my petticoats . . .'

'No need!' Thankful for the foresight that had caused her to pack the whisky and the remainder of the sheet used to bind Tom Gillon's arm, Alexa set to work. Carefully, she followed Harriet's directions, first cleansing the wound with whisky as she had seen her friend do.

'Dear God, let Jonathan be right,' she prayed as she poured the spirit with a liberal hand. 'Please, let him be right.'

Harriet was in great pain. Her breathing was laboured and beads of perspiration stood on her forehead, but she remained conscious until Alexa had applied the final bandage and then she passed out.

Alexa's heart thumped with fear as she poured water on to a kerchief and sponged Harriet's lips and forehead. Her friend lay so still and silent, so lifeless. She looked in desperation for Tom Gillon, but he was nowhere in sight.

'Will she be all right?' Mr Madoc asked anxiously.

'Mrs Symonds is badly hurt! We've got to get her to a doctor!'

'Where will we find a doctor out here?'

'I don't know, but we must find one. Where is Mr Gillon?'

He made a vague gesture in the direction of the fleeing villains. 'He went after them—I hope nothing's happened to him. Shall I go and look?'

The idea of the poor, vague Mr Madoc wandering around in the brush alarmed Alexa. 'Please stay. We'll need your protection if those ruffians return.'

This seemed to put resolve into the old gentleman, but Alexa was too distracted to notice. Harriet was still unconscious. Her pulse was uneven, and her breathing laboured.

There was a distant shot and a crashing in the undergrowth and they looked up fearfully, but it was Tom who eventually emerged leading one of the horses.

'They got the other,' he said. 'I couldn't stop them, but I managed to rescue this fellow.' He patted the white blaze on the gelding's nose with great satisfaction. Then he caught sight of Harriet and his smile died.

'I didn't know anyone was hurt. Oh, poor Harriet! Is it very bad?'

'We must get her to a doctor, Tom! Without proper care, she could die!'

CHAPTER NINE

Tom adjusted the harness to accommodate the remaining horse. Then they made Harriet as comfortable as possible on the seat. Alexa and Mrs Madoc crouched on the floor of the carriage, and the men sat on the box.

They had not gone far before they encountered a bullock cart loaded with fugitives. All had harrowing tales to tell, but also tales of great kindness. They were making haste for Kurnaul and urged the party in the carriage to join them.

Alexa and Tom knew that racing across country would prove dangerous for Harriet. It risked re-opening her wound and she had already lost too much blood. It was much safer to proceed at a steady pace. Neither would leave Harriet so, regretfully, they declined the offer.

Mr and Mrs Madoc, however, decided to go and were found room in the cart. The driver plied a whip and the double-yoked oxen broke into a run, trailing a cloud of dust in its wake.

It was cooler now as the sun moved down the sky and the carriage made good progress until it was too dark to see the road.

Although they had sometimes glimpsed riders in the distance and men on foot, they were not molested. The country through which they passed was particularly deserted, but they knew their luck couldn't last for ever.

'We'll rest now and continue at moon-rise,' Tom Gillon said. 'There's still some distance to go, but the closer we come to Kurnaul, the safer we'll be.'

They had moved off the road and now travelled some distance out on the plain parallel with it. Twice they glimpsed bands of riders galloping with abandon, their wild, excited cries loud in the night.

In the early dawn, a number of men on foot were seen trotting along the road, blazing torches held aloft. Many were armed with carbines and several were in the white uniform of the sepoy.

Tom stopped the carriage, a stationary object being less noticeable, and the travellers breathed a sigh of relief as the men trotted into the distance.

'We must find concealment before it's fully light,' Tom said. 'The horse needs rest, and there's too much activity now for us to travel safely by day.'

Alexa protested. In her concern for Harriet, she was prepared to take the chance and make a run for the British lines. But as the light strengthened, she could see that the jolting of the carriage had caused Harriet's wound to bleed again and realised that the older woman couldn't survive without some respite.

'Very well. We'll tie up and try for Kurnaul

tonight.'

Tom led the horse towards a wooded grove just visible in the dawning. As they approached, Alexa drew his attention to two small boys silhouetted on a rocky outcrop who had paused in driving a herd of goats to watch the carriage.

'Unfortunate,' Tom said, 'but it doesn't mean they'll betray us. They probably won't return to their village until nightfall. By then we'll be on our way.'

Despite his reassuring words, his expression was grim as he looked back over the way they had come.

The grove was larger than it appeared and in its centre was a small clearing and a tumble-down hut. They approached cautiously, found the hut long abandoned, and decided that it was perfect for their purpose.

While Alexa cleared the worst of the debris from the floor and fashioned a couch for Harriet from the cushions, Tom hid the vehicle in the thick brush behind the hut. Then he went back to the plain to cut fodder for the horse, which he'd housed in a crude lean-to beside the hut.

Alexa re-bandaged Harriet's shoulder, relieved to find that the bleeding had stopped and although the wound was inflamed, there was no sign yet of putrefaction.

'There, dear friend, that's all I can do,' she whispered.

When Tom returned, Alexa insisted on re-dressing his wounded arm, noting with relief that it was beginning to heal. They shared one of the remaining chapattis and drank a little water. Then they rested, taking turns to watch.

Alexa went frequently to attend Harriet, and when the fierce heat of the afternoon began to fade, was rewarded when her friend's eyelids fluttered and opened and the hazel eyes looked up at her with recognition.

'Alexandra,' Harriet's voice whispered. 'What is all this?'

'Hush, dear!' Alexa said. 'You were injured when we were attacked in the mango grove, but we are well on our way to Kurnaul. Now, drink as much as you can, then rest. Gather your strength for the journey.'

Under her friend's urging, Harriet managed to drink almost a full cup of water, but would eat nothing, and shortly afterwards, lapsed into unconsciousness. Her pulse, however, had steadied and her breathing was more regular.

'How is she, Alexa?' Tom asked when she joined him at the door.

'Improved, I think, but still in desperate need of a doctor. How soon can we set out again?'

He was silent and she looked at him sharply. 'What is it?'

'I've just examined the horse,' he said heavily. 'He's lame. A thorn has festered in his offside hoof. I've removed it and drained the

126

abscess, but it's too inflamed for him to travel, particularly pulling the carriage. I should have noticed it sooner. It's my fault, and I'm sorry!'

She looked at him angrily. 'How could you be so careless? You know how important it is to get Harriet to a doctor! We've got to go tonight—if we have to drag the carriage ourselves!'

He looked unhappily into her indignant face. 'You're prepared to do that?'

'I'm prepared to try, if it's the only way she can be moved. We can't just do nothing and let Harriet die. She's a dear friend!'

The reporter said softly, 'Alexa, you are quite a woman. But no matter how much we'd like to, we won't get far drawing the carriage ourselves.' He thought a moment. 'Have we any money? There must be a village nearby. I'll risk it just before dusk and see if I can purchase a horse or a mule.'

'There's five hundred rupees in my satchel.'

'Two hundred will be more than enough.'

Alexa gave him the money plus an extra fifty rupees which he concealed in his shoe. She also gave him an apology.

'I'm sorry, Tom! It isn't your fault—the horse going lame. We'd have been in dire straights without you. You will be careful, won't you? If the village looks hostile, please don't risk it. We'll find another way!'

For answer, he bent and kissed her cheek.

The sun was past its zenith as the reporter

made preparations to leave, fastening the empty water bottle to his belt in expectation of filling it at the village well. There was less than half a bottle left and that was for Harriet.

As Tom's slight figure vanished into the trees, Alexa went outside to sit on some logs stacked near the door, and wait anxiously for his return.

They had remained concealed inside the hut all day for fear that the young goat-herds had betrayed them, but the hours had passed peacefully and it seemed certain now that they would be safe until morning.

But she had scarcely settled when she heard the sound of horses' hooves. Deeply alarmed, she took refuge again in the hut, taking up the long knife that Tom Gillon had retrieved from the dead ruffian in the mango grove. She stood guard beside Harriet's couch, prepared to defend her friend with all her might.

Crouched in the shadows inside the doorway, she waited, heart hammering with fear. A horse broke cover and started across the open ground; on its back not one but two riders. The first, a young man in the uniform of a Cornet of Horse—the second, a man in civilian clothing whose identity was concealed until he slid from his place behind the saddle.

Then, Alexa dropped the knife, lifted her skirts high and ran. 'James,' she cried. 'Oh, James,' and flung herself in joyous relief upon the newcomer.

As always in the tropics, the darkness came quickly. No light infiltrated the hut, but there were candle-lamps on the carriage and one of these with its reflecting mirrors illuminated the interior quite brightly.

After extracting every detail of the flight from Delhi and Harriet's injury, James told of his own adventures.

'I had just reached the Company office when I heard gunfire from the direction of the Rajghat Gate,' he said. 'Knowing of the threatened mutiny at Meerut, I could guess the cause. I informed the General Manager and he ordered the evacuation of the building. Everyone was free to return to their homes and take whatever steps necessary to protect their families. I set out at once for the Symonds' house, but the way was barred by armed mobs who were attacking every European they saw. Some troops had been brought in to oppose them, but not nearly enough. The fighting was fierce and there were many dead and injured in the streets.

'I turned one way and another, seeking a passage to the Amritsar Road. Then, in a back alley, I came across this young fellow besieged by half a dozen of the scoundrels. He was fighting like a demon, armed with an Arabian scimitar that he had gotten from goodness knows where.'

James motioned toward his companion who grinned cheerfully. 'I looted a curio shop actually. My pistol was stolen the previous night while I slept.'

'You are Cornet Bradley, aren't you?' Alexa said, recalling the young man's face. 'If you remember, we danced at the King of Delhi's Grand Ball.'

The youngster had recognised her instantly despite her tattered appearance. He bowed gallantly. 'I'm flattered that you remember me, Miss Denton.'

James interrupted impatiently. 'After we'd seen the scoundrels off, we decided to leave the city and ride around the perimeter until we could enter by the Kashmir Gate and so reach you and Harriet. But we'd underestimated the extent of the uprising. The city was full of mutineers. Every sepoy from Meerut seemed to be there, and more were arriving every hour. Ruffians from the bazaars were joining with them and our way was blocked at every turn. We barely escaped with our lives and had to flee across the plain to escape.'

'Mr Brunswick's horse was injured and we had to leave it and ride double,' Cornet Bradley contributed. He was watching as Alexa tucked a shawl about Harriet and moistened her mouth with water. 'Forgive me, but do you have any of that stuff to spare?'

'I'm afraid not, but when Mr Gillon comes back there will be enough for us all.' Alexa rose to her feet and looked at James who was restlessly pacing the hut with an agitation quite foreign to his usual controlled manner. 'How did you find us?' she asked.

'Luck! We came to a friendly village. A man told us of seeing a carriage carrying several Europeans driving along the road toward the west. We had no idea at that time that it was your party, of course.'

'And we had no idea we'd been seen,' Alexa said ruefully.

'More than once. Two women cutting rushes saw you fork left near the river crossing. Some children saw you on the road, and a youth saw you enter a mango grove at noon. We found bloodstained ground and this—' James held out a brooch fashioned in the shape of a dragonfly.

Alexa's hand went to her neck. 'It's mine! I hadn't even missed it!'

James held it out to her and when she reached for it, caught her hand. 'Can you imagine my feelings when I recognised it as yours?' he asked grimly. 'Alexa, I was so afraid for you.'

'It was poor Harriet who was hurt. And the robbers! Tom Gillon was wonderful! He kept his head—acted so coolly. He saved us all!'

'No doubt!' James said shortly. 'Anyway, we ran into an armed band and were chased over half Bengal. It took half a day to find your tracks again and that was due to some goatherds who saw you enter this wood.'

'I'm pleased that not everyone has turned

against us,' Alexa said quietly. 'My parents regard India as their second home. They had many good friends among the native population. It would break their hearts to think that not one of them thought kindly of us.'

'It was those damned cartridges! And the stupidity of the Government.'

James turned back to Alexa and took her face in his hands. For a moment, she feared he would kiss her, but he just stared down into her eyes. 'We'll soon be out of here,' he said and, turning on his heel, left the hut.

There was a thumping and crackling from behind the hut and realising that James was breaking out the carriage, Cornet Bradley went to help.

When Alexa went out, she could see in the moonlight that they had harnessed the cavalry horse to the shafts and James was speaking earnestly to the young officer.

James caught sight of her and came across the clearing. He took her arm.

'Come, Alexa, the carriage is ready. We must make haste for Kurnaul.'

'We can't leave until Mr Gillon returns, James. He's been gone over an hour and should be back shortly.'

'If he hasn't been killed!'

'Please, don't say that! I feel sure he's all right!'

James made an impatient gesture. 'Even if

he is, we've seen the last of him! I know Tom Gillon! With money in his pocket and a horse beneath him, he'll be well on his way. You were insane to trust him with so much.'

'That's a scandalous accusation, James. Tom saved our lives.'

'And now he's saving his own. Alexa, this is no time to argue. Come!' He pulled urgently on her arm and she suddenly realised his true intent.

'Surely, you don't mean to leave Harriet? Help me to lift her into the carriage. Perhaps Mr Bradley—Where is Mr Bradley?'

He laughed sardonically. 'I've sent him to watch for Gillon's return. As for Harriet Symonds, she would only slow us down. We've got to travel fast if we're to make Kurnaul by dawn.'

She looked up at him, appalled by his callous tone. 'Harriet's our friend, James! She's badly hurt. We can't leave her!'

'Don't be foolish, Alexa,' he said sharply. 'The two of us can make good speed. We'll send help back when we reach the lines.'

'I can't believe you are serious, James. If we're caught there'll be no escape for those left here. We could be condemning them to death.' Her voice strengthened. 'We must go together. The carriage will hold us all.'

'And we'll be caught and cut to pieces. I've no intention of leaving my bones out on that plain, or yours either!' Grasping her waist, he began to drag her over to the carriage. 'Get in. We've wasted enough time.'

Furiously, Alexa fought him, kicking and struggling. 'You mustn't do this!'

'Get in, Alexa.' He lifted her bodily and she beat at his face with her clenched fists. Something in him seemed to snap. 'Get in, damn you!'

She was afraid to scream, knowing how sound travels at night, but in desperation she twisted and caught the iron wheel-rim and hung on.

James made one last effort to force Alexa into the carriage, but she resisted with all her might and abruptly he let her go.

'Very well—but you had the chance, Alexa. Never say you didn't.'

Realising that nothing would deflect him from his purpose, she cried, 'Go, James, if you must, but please leave the carriage. Take the horse—it will be quicker in the end.'

He gestured impatiently. 'Time's wasting! Stand back!' And ignoring her pleas, he leaped on to the driving seat and snatched up the reins.

'Here,' Alexa cried, throwing her engagement ring at him. 'Take back your ring. There is nothing between us now, James, nothing.'

The horse was dancing nervously, unsettled by the scuffle. James plied the whip, cracking it expertly above the animal's ears. Startled, it leaped forward and another crack sent it racing from the clearing.

It was very dark beneath the trees and Alexa held her breath, waiting for a crash, but the beat of the hooves continued until they faded into the night.

Almost sobbing with anger, Alexa stood in the soft darkness fighting to regain her composure. She felt betrayed and outraged and very afraid.

This hiding place would not remain secret for long. The goat-herds had talked once, they would talk again. But James was a survivor. He would make it to Kurnaul and send back help! He'd promised—and she had to believe him.

Somewhere in the night a bird screeched. There was a startled flapping of wings and then silence. Alexa gave an involuntary cry of fear.

'Miss Denton? It's me, Daniel Bradley!'

Alexa almost fainted with relief as she recognised the Cornet of Horse as he loomed out of the darkness into the bright moonlight.

'No sign of Mr Gillon, I'm afraid. I don't know how long Mr Brunswick wants me to watch.' He looked about him. 'Where is Mr Brunswick?'

Alexa said heavily, 'Mr Brunswick has taken the carriage and your horse and is, no doubt, well on his way to Kurnaul.'

The officer's boyish face puckered into a frown. 'I understood that the carriage was to

135

carry Mrs Symonds.'

'I'm afraid you were deceived, as I was, Mr Bradley. I must see to my friend.'

Heavy hearted, Alexa turned and walked towards the hut.

He followed on her heels and leaned against the door post as Alexa kneeled beside the unconscious woman.

As she worked, she told Daniel of James's departure. 'He's gone to send help. And a doctor,' she added quickly as an oath escaped Bradley's lips.

'You don't believe that,' a voice as soft as falling leaves whispered. Alexa gave a cry of joy as she saw that Harriet's eyes were open and intelligent.

'Harriet, dear Harriet—no, don't try to talk. Rest, save your strength.'

Harriet motioned and Alexa put her ear close to her lips.

'He won't dare send help,' Harriet said. 'No-one must know he ran away!'

'Perhaps he'll turn back for us,' Alexa said.

'If he does,' the young Cornet of Horse said, grimly fingering the hilt of his scimitar, 'I shall run him through for cowardice.'

CHAPTER TEN

The moon was well up when Alexa heard a whispered challenge from Daniel Bradley who was on watch. She hurried outside to see a man leading a horse across the clearing. Tom Gillon had returned!

Overwhelmed with relief, she ran to embrace him. 'Thank goodness you are safely back. We were afraid something bad had happened.'

'Sorry it took so long. The nearest village had no horses, but one of the men agreed to take me to another village where one was for sale—at an exorbitant price. I also bought food, blankets and water gourds and paid very dearly. I'm afraid there's little left of the two hundred rupees.'

'Cheap at twice the price! But you haven't met Cornet Daniel Bradley.'

She introduced the two, explaining how the youngster came to join them. Feeling embarrassed and somehow responsible, Alexa went on to relate how James had driven off in the carriage.

'I should have stopped him, Tom. By the time I realised he really meant to drive away, it was too late.'

'You are in no way to blame, Alexa! Brunswick is responsible for his own actions, and must live with his own conscience. Let's hope he has enough decency to send help.'

'My sentiments exactly, sir,' Cornet Bradley said. 'Do you think we can eat now? You did say you'd brought food and water, didn't you, Mr Gillon?'

The three sat outside on the wood pile where their voices wouldn't disturb Harriet who had fallen into a deep sleep. Hungrily, they devoured the fried chicken and curried rice that Tom had brought, saving the most tender pieces to tempt the invalid should she recover sufficiently.

'As I see it,' Tom said, 'we can't wait around in the hope that Brunswick will send help. The news of our presence will be common knowledge in the nearby villages. It's only a matter of time before it reaches hostile ears.'

Alexa put aside her empty plate. 'Our only hope is for one of you to take the horse. There'll be army patrols out by now and you might come up with one. Otherwise, you must try for Kurnaul.'

Tom Gillon cleared his throat. 'The horse is small but sturdy, capable of carrying two—'

'You and Miss Denton must go,' Daniel interrupted.

'So I propose,' Tom continued as if Daniel hadn't spoken, 'that the two of you leave immediately.'

Bradley stood up. 'I am a soldier, sir,' he said stiffly. 'It's my duty to remain and protect

138

Mrs Symonds!'

'I applaud your courage, Cornet! But you are younger and lighter, and the logical choice.'

'Younger I may be, but not lighter, Mr Gillon. You and Miss Denton will go.'

Alexa put her tin cup down with a little slam. 'Please stop arguing, gentlemen. It's getting nowhere and time is passing. I have no intention of leaving my friend! The two of you can ride double!'

There was an outburst of protests but Alexa was firm. She wouldn't leave Harriet. Neither would the men leave her unprotected, so in the end they drew straws. The short one fell to Cornet Bradley.

Reluctantly, the young officer mounted the little horse and with a water bottle and some rice on his saddle, bid them goodbye. Alexa went to his side and looked up at him, a boyish silhouette in the moonlight.

'Daniel, you are going into danger,' she said quietly. 'May I kiss you goodbye, for the sake of your mother?'

A sudden brilliance came into his eyes. Then he bent and she embraced him.

'Don't worry about me, Miss Denton,' he said straightening resolutely in the saddle. 'I'll get through safely and return with a relief troop.'

Then the youth turned the horse and cantered out on to the moonlit plain.

Alexa went inside to sit with Harriet and Tom followed her. He looked down at the sleeping woman. 'Her colour is better, I believe!'

'Do you think so?' Alexa whispered. 'Oh, if only we had a doctor!'

'No-one could have looked after her better, Alexa. Now you must get some sleep. You're exhausted and we can't have two invalids! I'll keep watch.'

She smiled at the small, slight, middle-aged man. 'You've been a rock, Tom! We couldn't have managed without you. You've been splendid!'

He flushed, pleased and embarrassed by the praise. 'Saving my own neck, too, remember. And think what a story I'll have when it's over!'

Alexa lay down near Harriet, covering herself with one of the blankets.

The reporter draped another about his shoulders and took up position on the wood pile. He, too, was almost exhausted and despite his resolve, dozed as he leaned back against the hut wall.

Shouts woke Alexa and she struggled from a deep sleep, confused by her surroundings and the alien noise. She got to her feet as men burst through the narrow doorway, their voices reverberating in the narrow confines of the hut.

Wild oaths in Hindustani swept the

140

confusion from her mind as rough hands seized her. Shock gave her strength and she fought so desperately that she broke free and almost reached Harriet before she was caught again.

By the flickering light of the candle, she saw a man poised above the prone form of her friend, a long blade held above his head as he prepared to strike.

'No!' Alexa's anguished scream tore the night.

The sound seemed to rouse Harriet and she opened her eyes and stared up at the would-be assassin poised above her. The man with the blade laughed, repositioned, raised the weapon higher.

In the sudden silence, all eyes stared at the gleaming blade. Alexa thought that her heart would stop with the sheer terror of it!

Suddenly, a new voice shouted in Hindustani. 'Stop!' And then the candle went out, leaving the hut in total darkness.

In the following confusion of sound and movement, Alexa was dragged, almost thrown, from the hut. Someone pulled her away from her captor and she was thrust across the clearing.

It was almost dawn. The sky in the east was streaked with vermilion and as her eyes grew accustomed to the dim light she saw the white uniform of her captor, and the two stripes that identified him as a naik, a corporal of sepoys.

Once, she would have looked to such a man for protection, but knew she could expect nothing now. This, then, was the end.

Proudly she lifted her chin. 'Kill me if you must! Why do you hesitate?'

'Be quiet if you want to live,' he hissed. 'But know that I do not do this for you—I do it for my wife, Seeta.'

'You are Seeta's husband!' She looked at the dim figure, a wild hope stirring in her heart. Hysteria was not far away.

'I can protect you only because these are my men, but when others join us, I make no promises.'

'I thank you for my life, but what of my friends?'

'They are not hurt!' he replied quietly. 'Now, be silent!'

Alexa trembled with relief.

The NCO motioned to one of the men who tied her wrists with rope and she offered no resistance.

They were carrying Harriet from the hut on a litter made from branches and blankets. She was conscious. 'Alexandra,' she called, her voice just strong enough to reach Alexa's ears. 'Alexandra, where are you?'

'I'm here, Harriet! Don't worry—lie still—save your strength.'

Her captor shouted for silence and she was pushed towards the path. Tom joined her. There was blood on his forehead and his jacket was torn, flapping as he stumbled before the prodding of the mutineers. But they were all alive!

They came out on to the plain as the rising sun began to burn away the dew so that the harsh landscape shimmered in a gossamer mist of pale orange.

In high spirits, the mutineers laughed and sang as they headed west, pushing their captives before them, mocking them as they stumbled over the rough ground. Alexa tried not to mind for they carried Harriet's litter with good humour and had even rigged shade for the sick woman. She was anxious not to upset them in any way.

As the sun climbed higher, thirst became a real problem for the water was in the hands of the mutineers. In the end, Alexa risked approaching Seeta's husband and humbly begged for water for Harriet, who was obviously suffering.

'She is sorely hurt and in need of the famed chivalry of the sepoys.'

The naik stared down at the woman on the litter. Alexa thought he would refuse for a kind of anger crossed his face. But the anger was against himself that he hadn't the stomach to punish these hapless foreigners as they surely deserved. Abruptly, he mentioned to one of his men before turning away. The prisoners were each given a cup of water, and refreshed, they carried on.

But the mood had changed. The mutineers marched silently over the baked, trackless terrain. They no longer joked. They were sullen as they harried the prisoners and there was spite in the cuffs and shoves.

As she stumbled along, Alexa's frightened eyes met Tom's and she saw that he was also frightened by the change of mood.

At noon, they came to a depression grown with low scrub and stunted trees. Here, the NCO halted his band. The two captives were thrust on to the ground beside a tree and the litter was dropped carelessly beside them.

Their captors flung themselves down in the shade and began to share the savoury contents of a terracotta pot.

Alexa crouched beside Harriet who was awake and uncomplaining. She even managed a smile and whispered 'Chin up, Alexandra!'

Alexa examined the bandages, relieved to find that there was no fresh bleeding. Her skin was dry and hot, however, and there was a feverish light in her eyes. And she was dehydrating.

The men were drinking freely from the water bottles while they examined the contents of Harriet's bag and Alexa's satchel, laughing at the photographs and squabbling over the money.

When the men didn't offer any of the precious liquid to their prisoners, Alexa felt a tremendous anger. Instinct told her not to ask again for water, but she couldn't stop herself. However, she had the sense to go humbly.

'Please, in the name of humanity, I again beg for water for my sick friend.'

The mutineers stopped drinking and thirteen pairs of eyes turned upon Alexa with open hostility. Several made to rise, but the NCO forestalled them by springing to his feet and with a sweep of his hand knocked her to the ground.

Immediately, Tom Gillon leaped up and rushed to her defence. He grappled with the naik and, despite his slight frame, bore him down by the very fury of his rush. The other sepoys yelled with excitement and joined the fray.

Tom could do no more than coil defensively. The mutineers howled with glee, giving in at last to the violence that stemmed from their irreversible act of mutiny. And it was their undoing, for they failed to see the dust cloud moving fast over the plain, a big white horse at its head, failed to hear the pounding of hooves and jingle of accoutrements, until it was too late.

A warning shout went up, but before the sepoys could properly deploy, the blue-coated dragoons poured over the rim of the depression, their great horses steaming with the speed of the charge. The mutineers could do no more than offer a ragged, unco-ordinated defence. The fight was fierce but short-lived. With bewildering rapidity, the sepoys were overwhelmed.

When the guns were quiet and the ring of metal upon metal had ceased, and the shouting had died away, an officer detached himself from the scene and strode over to where Alexa and Tom crouched defensively beside Harriet's litter.

'Thank goodness we got here in time.' It was Gideon Masters! And he pulled Alexa into his arms. He held her close for a long moment as she clung to him in joyous thanksgiving. Then, he gently released her. He gripped Tom Gillon's shoulder encouragingly before kneeling beside the woman on the litter. 'Hold fast, Harriet. Ambulances are coming and a very special medic with them!'

'Jonathan?' Harriet whispered. 'Gideon, you pirate, say it's Jonathan!'

'Who else?' He laughed. 'Now drink some water. All of you.'

He gave a full bottle to Alexa, but as she helped her friend to drink, she trembled with the reaction of the sudden release from danger.

Wagons were arriving and medical orderlies, and the tall, slight figure of the Surgeon Major who bent over Harriet with a tenderness that threatened to do what the mutineers had failed to do, reduce the three fugitives to tears.

As one of the orderlies tended to Tom's

bruised and battered features, Gideon picked Alexa up in his arms and with her head cradled against his broad shoulder, carried her out of the hollow to where the ambulances waited. Gently, he laid her on one of the couches beneath the hooped, canvas canopy.

She had longed for him with such intensity that now he was actually here, she felt strangely shy, 'How did you find us?'

'We can thank a young Cornet of Horse who came riding up to our patrol with a dozen yelling ruffians hard on his heels.'

She laughed with relief. 'Daniel Bradley! Is he all right?'

'He is surely the hero of the hour! He told us exactly where to find you and then it was simply a matter of tracking you across the plain.'

She gazed up at him as he leaned over her. The angles of his strong face had softened and there was a light in his eyes that sent the colour flooding into her cheeks. She desperately wanted him to hold her again.

'Gideon, I—' But she was not to finish for the orderlies brought Harriet's stretcher which was placed upon the opposite couch. Tom Gillon climbed into the second ambulance together with three wounded sepoys. Then the troop set out for Kurnaul.

The swaying of the wagon soon lulled the two women to sleep, and Jonathan watched over them. Neither stirred when the column diverted to an outlying village where no less than eleven fugitives had found refuge. Nor were they aware that the column moved steadily on through the night.

Alexa woke when the ambulance stopped before the garrison hospital. As she alighted, she looked about for Gideon and glimpsed him at the head of his troop as they trotted away. She felt a keen disappointment that he should go without a word.

Then she caught sight of some prisoners, survivors of the fight in the hollow, being marched away across the square. She looked around and seeing Jonathan close by, went over to him.

'Jonathan, that naik is Seeta's husband,' she said pointing. 'He spared our lives, and I believe he saved mine a second time when I asked for water and his men seemed about to attack me. He knocked me down before they could act, but didn't hurt me. Will you speak for him, Jonathan?'

'Yes, of corse I will. I'll see that the general hears of it.'

After a brief medical examination, which found her fit and well, Alexa luxuriated in a cool bath. Then, in borrowed clothes and with her newly-washed hair piled in shining profusion on her head, she went into the wards.

First she visited Tom Gillon who had been prescribed twenty-four hours bed rest. Despite his bruised and battered appearance, she found him cheerful and well, and already composing a story for the *London Telegraph*.

She left him to it and went in to see Harriet. In a pretty nightgown and pristine bandages, Harriet already looked better—perhaps the presence of her husband had much to do with that.

'It's wonderful to see you looking so much better, Harriet.'

Jonathan, who was unashamedly holding his wife's hand, said, 'I've heard from Tom Gillon of all you did for Harriet, Alexa. You stood by her and kept her alive and I'm more grateful than words can say.'

'I only did what I could,' Alexa said briskly. 'Tom was splendid, and so was young Bradley. But it's over now and Harriet must concentrate on getting well.'

There was a pause during which Jonathan studied a crack in the wall. He said gruffly, 'The Waldicotts are here, by the way. And I, er, hear that James Brunswick came in a few days ago. Took off again almost at once for Bombay.'

'Did he—did he mention our predicament at all?'

'Apparently not. I'm so very sorry, Alexa.'

'Don't be,' Harriet said briskly. 'James and Alexandra were never suited. She's better without him. Besides, her heart is elsewhere.'

Colour burned in Alexa's cheeks as Harriet

added, 'Anyone with half an eye can see she dotes on Gideon Masters.'

Jonathan's brows rose higher. 'I spoke to the lieutenant no more than ten minutes ago. He's just leaving for Rawalpindi.'

The rest of Jonathan's words went over Alexa's head. She was staring at Harriet in wide-eyed dismay.

'Go, Alexandra, quickly!'

Alexa needed no further bidding. Lifting her skirts high, she fled out of the open doors and across the wide, dusty parade ground to the west gate. To her horror, Gideon's troops were already out on the plain, their blue coats bright in the sunshine.

She ran after them, her voice crying on the wind, 'Gideon, wait! Wait for me!'

It seemed he wouldn't hear and, breathless, she stopped, almost sobbing with despair. Then a white horse wheeled from the head of the column and came galloping back to where she stood.

He swung from the saddle and she flung herself on him. 'Take me with you,' she pleaded. 'Please, Gideon, take me with you!'

He held her from him, looked searchingly into her face. And what he saw there brought a smile to his lips and a happy gleam to his eyes.

'Darling girl,' he said softly. 'I heard how Brunswick deserted you, but are you sure you're over him?'

'As sure as the sun rises and sets! I was over

James long before he drove away in our carriage.' Shyly she added, 'I love you, Gideon, truly, deeply, with all my heart. I want to be with you always—if you'll have me.'

His lips gave her the answer she longed for. 'But I warn you,' he said, when he drew back. 'If you come with me now, I won't ever let you go!'

He swung back into the saddle and as he lifted her up behind him, she saw the lavender ribbon that she had given to the red knight at the tournament in Lucknow tied about his forearm.

'My lady's favour,' he said, touching it. 'You were destined to be my lady, Alexa, from the first moment I saw you in the parlour at Whitmore Square.'

She held tight around his waist as the big white horse moved out across the burning plain towards the distant hills. Contentedly resting her head against Gideon's broad back, Alexa knew that she would love this man for ever. That she would never leave him or the wide, beautiful land that was India . . .

We hope you have enjoyed this Large Print book. Other Chivers Press or Thorndike Press Large Print books are available at your library or directly from the publishers.

For more information about current and forthcoming titles, please call or write, without obligation, to:

Chivers Press Limited
Windsor Bridge Road
Bath BA2 3AX
England
Tel. (01225) 335336

OR

G.K. Hall & Co.
295 Kennedy Memorial Drive
Waterville
Maine 04901
USA

All our Large Print titles are designed for easy reading, and all our books are made to last.